Rachel's Dancing Dream

by

Rissa Poloway

ISBN 978-0-7414-2551-5

Cover artwork by Benjamin Juliá

Published by:

PUBLISHING.COM

Info@buybooksontheweb.com
www.buybooksontheweb.com
Toll-free (877) BUY BOOK
Local Phone (610) 941-9999
Fax (610) 941-9959

Printed in the United States of America

Published November 2012

With love to my parents, Deborah and Benjamin Simpson,
and my husband, Sigmund Poloway.

Acknowledgments

For their tireless encouragement and support along this journey, special thanks to my daughter, Merel Poloway Juliá, my son and his wife, Mark and Susan Poloway, my sister, Sharon Arbittier, and my four grandsons, Sam, David, Raúl, and notably Benjamin, who created the artwork on the cover.

I extend my deepest appreciation to my editor, Victoria Wright, for her incalculable help and guidance throughout the publishing process. Also thanks to Professor Sally-Anne Milgrim for her insightful input. My colleague, June Buffington King has my undying gratitude for her friendship, encouragement, and help through the years. Also, many thanks to her husband, Dick King, for his patience in getting me started with the book.

CHAPTER ONE

One week before Rachel's eleventh birthday, her father held two tickets in the air and said to her, "Here is your birthday present. Little dancer, you and I are going to the *Swan Lake* ballet next Wednesday night."

Rachel was ecstatic—a warmth filled her from head to toe, spilling out into squeals of delight. "Oh, oh, how wonderful!" she exclaimed. She knew the story and the music of *Swan Lake* by heart, because her parents had given her the record on her last birthday. Since then she had played it on the Victrola and danced to it every day.

Mama had grumbled over and over. "Rachel, forget this ballerina business. This is the Depression. Dancing is for rich people, not poor Jewish immigrants like us."

But Rachel looked up from reading and rereading the date and seat numbers of the tickets in her hand, and she saw that Mama's blue eyes were misty, her smile tender.

"What about me?" asked her nine-year-old sister, Bronna, pouting because she wasn't included.

"Yeah! Me, too!" said her brother, Hyman. He was almost two years older than Rachel and insisted that he hated dancing.

Mama silenced them, answering firmly, "We can't all go. But Rachel loves dancing so much—it's a special birthday treat. Enough talk. Eat."

Ever since she could remember, Rachel loved to dance. She took every book about dancing out of the library. Studying the pictures, she tried to copy the dance positions.

She couldn't wait to come home from Hebrew class, which she attended every day after public school, to dance to her *Swan Lake* record. It was her greatest treasure. The music was always there deep inside her. It carried her down the street on tiptoes. It lifted her in giant leaps up the steps to the third-floor apartment where they lived.

The kitchen was her stage. Sink, icebox, stove, table, chairs, and brown leather lounge all faded from view as she danced. In front of the small mirror on the wall, thin, shy Rachel Sussman turned into a sleek, graceful swan, exactly like the ballerinas in the movies—their heads covered with snowy feathers, their eyes made up to shine like black diamonds, their faces white and haughty. She could scarcely believe that in a week all this would come alive on the stage.

She drifted through the days like a sleepwalker, waiting until the moment Papa would present their tickets to the usher, magical keys unlocking the door to her first ballet.

Wednesday morning finally came. "Happy Birthday!" Hyman and Bronna shouted. As Mama gave her a pat on the rump for each count, with an extra one for good luck, they sang out, "One, two, three, four, five, six, seven, eight, nine, ten, eleven...and twelve!" Hyman, who also insisted on giving her birthday pats, hit her harder and harder until his pats turned into slaps.

"You're hurting me," Rachel cried.

"Ahh, don't be sore," he joked, "I'm only kidding,"

She fidgeted through her classes, anticipating the evening ahead. The public school she and her brother and sister attended was across the street and the Hebrew school, which they went to afterward, was only a few doors from their dwelling, so she was home by five-thirty. Seeing how excited Rachel was, Mama permitted her to dress before supper. They always ate first and then got dressed, wearing their good clothes only when they actually went out the door. But tonight was special.

Rachel's wardrobe consisted of two cotton dresses that the downstairs neighbor's granddaughter had outgrown. The pink one with the white Peter Pan collar and short puffy sleeves was hanging on the door of the bedroom she and Bronna shared. Mama had washed and ironed it that very afternoon. Rachel carefully took off the blue polka-dot dress she'd worn to school, hanging it in the closet.

She went to the bathroom to wash, indulging herself afterward with a few liberal powderpuffs of Mama's Lilies Of The Valley Talcum. Then she hurriedly went back to the bedroom to put on a fresh undershirt, snuggies, petticoat, and high, brown lisle stockings with round, pink, elastic garters to hold them up. Then the dress. Because Mama's strenuous shoe polishing did not improve the shabby state of her old, brown oxfords, Rachel couldn't resist wishing that Mrs. Stein's granddaughter would outgrow a pair of black Mary Jane patent leathers with the strap buttoning at the ankle. Instantly she felt guilty and ungrateful. Her precious black ballet slippers, the only ones she ever possessed, were Mrs. Stein's granddaughter's castoffs. How could she ask for more?

Papa worked as an expressman, delivering stoves and heavy furniture with a horse and wagon. He left at five-thirty in the morning while everyone was asleep and didn't come home until eight in the evening, when they had supper. Mama insisted they wait for him. "Families eat together," she said emphatically.

Papa had promised Rachel he'd get home as soon as possible. When she finished dressing, she checked the battered cuckoo clock on the wall, listening worriedly to hear if it was still ticking. Time went so slowly. He arrived at exactly ten minutes after six, breathless from running up three flights of stairs. He put his long arms around Rachel in a bear hug and lifted her up to his six-foot height for a birthday kiss.

"Rachel, in your honor I'm home early," he said.

"Thank you, Papa," she whispered.

He quickly shaved, bathed, and took his black suit out from the back of his closet. It reeked of mothballs. Hyman held his nose at the peculiar camphor odor and rolled his eyes to the ceiling.

Supper was an ordeal. Rachel's favorite dish of brisket, potatoes, *kasha*, and gravy was practically untouched. She tried to nibble on the pumpernickel bread and garlic pickles but nothing went down. She couldn't even swallow the cold borsht drink. She made a pretense of playing with the food, hoping Mama wouldn't notice.

But Mama always noticed. At the top of the stairs, as she hugged Rachel and kissed her goodbye, she exclaimed, "Your hands are like ice!" Turning to Papa, she continued in a loud voice, "As if she's not skinny enough, she didn't eat a thing."

"Tomorrow she'll eat two suppers," said Papa.

"It's not funny," Mama said, her voice strident. "She's been in a daze all week. I don't know if it's a good idea taking her to the ballet."

Rachel edged to the door thinking, Oh, please, don't let them get into an argument now.

"She'll be all right," Papa reassured Mama. "Don't worry."

"Worry? I worry we're giving her false hopes. This will only make her want to dance more, and you know there is no money for lessons."

"Everything will work out, Dora," Papa smiled as he patted Mama's cheek. "Remember, you're the one who thought about saving money for the tickets in the first place."

Rachel was surprised. She couldn't figure Mama out. Always complaining about her dancing, yet she was the one responsible for the tickets. It was a puzzle.

Papa bent to kiss Hyman and Bronna goodbye.

"Rachel's sure lucky going out at nighttime," Hyman said. "You never take me out and I'm the oldest."

"It's not fair," said Bronna, her lower lip quivering.

"Again with the complaint department. We went through that already," said Mama sternly.

Rachel couldn't believe what she was hearing. Her mother always favored Hyman, the only son, and Bronna, the golden-haired baby. For Rachel to be singled out like this by her was a miracle. At this moment, Mama with her blue eyes and long, blonde hair tied in a knot at the nape of her neck, wearing a shapeless cotton dress and apron, changed before Rachel's eyes into a blue-eyed, blonde-haired angel.

Mama was transformed into her old self as she turned to Rachel and pointed her forefinger up in the air and then down at Rachel and said, "You better not give me any trouble getting up for school tomorrow." As she waved them off, Rachel thought that maybe Papa was glad to finally escape, too. Hurrying down the stairs, she heard Mama say in a low voice, "Have a good time."

Outside, yellow smoke from the chimneys of the brick row houses made circles in the night sky before vanishing in the biting February wind. Clinging tightly to Papa's hand, they waited for the trolley at the corner of Third and Catherine Streets, where they lived. Papa kept craning his neck to see if it was coming. Despite the cold, Rachel felt a fire within, looking at Papa so tall and handsome all dressed up, and anticipating the night in store. Luckily, after a few minutes of waiting they heard the clang of the trolley. She was so excited that the ride to the Forrest Theater at Eleventh and Walnut Streets, almost seventeen blocks, seemed short. As the trolley slowed for the stop, Papa said, "Now you'll see why this theater is considered one of the most beautiful in Philadelphia."

She nodded her head. As they descended the trolley steps, she saw the great building, its brilliant lights shining on the surrounding buildings.

As her father led Rachel through the crowd, she noticed that although it was a weeknight, many people were dressed in formal attire. She saw men stroking their mustaches, and tipping their hats. She saw women wearing furs, satins, and glittering jewels. She could smell different perfumes every few steps she took.

Why, they're all like kings and queens! Rachel thought. She tried to cover the elbow patch on her frayed winter coat, though Mama always insisted it was invisible. She was glad when the usher finally led them to their seats high in the upper balcony.

5

"Are we too far away? Can you see the stage?" Papa asked, bending his head toward her.

"Oh, Papa, it's wonderful," Rachel said. He looked tired sitting beside her, and under the bright light she saw a pulse throbbing in his neck and realized he was excited, too. He had told her many times how he had once seen the great Pavlova dance.

He squeezed Rachel's hand, and looked down at her with the brown eyes that were just like hers. He said reverently, as though for the first time, "You know, Tchai-kovsky, the composer of *Swan Lake*, was a Russian. And so was Pavlova. Some people even said she was Jewish. They called her The Incomparable One. I saw her dance once, you know. I'll never forget that."

The overheated theater drew out the unmistakable odor of mothballs from Papa's suit. Although he was oblivious to it, the people around them sniffed audibly. But it didn't matter to Rachel. Nothing mattered except that she was with Papa at the ballet.

The rustling noises hushed as the lights dimmed. Far below them in the orchestra pit, the conductor raised his baton. The glorious music she knew so well from her record filled the theatre with the overture. Rachel pressed her hands against her heart as the curtain slowly rose and, right before her eyes, the magic began to unfold. Through music and dance she was transported to a land where swans glided in the moonlight, sorcerers plotted evil, and princes and princesses died for love.

Rothbart, an evil magician, casts his spells upon a group of maidens and changes them into swans who can only appear in their human forms during the hours from midnight to dawn. Only the power of a young male's sworn love can set a chosen one free. Prince Siegfried, hunting in the woods, meets Odette, Queen of the Swans, and falls in love with her. She tells him the sad tale and how the spell can be broken. He swears eternal love and asks her to come to the ball at the castle the next night, at which his mother has decided he must choose a wife.

The magician arrives at the ball with his daughter Odile, whom he has transformed to look like Odette. Thinking it is she, Siegfried tells his mother this is the person he intends to marry and swears his love for her, while Odette, entrapped as a swan until midnight, flutters helplessly against the window of the ballroom. Siegfried, discovering his terrible mistake, rushes to the lake to find Odette, but because he has broken his vow to her, she is now condemned to remain under the power of the magician forever. The lovers decide that if they cannot be together in life, they choose death, and throw themselves into the lake and drown. However, the power of their love defeats Rothbart, crouched high on a rock. He stumbles and falls, crashing fatally to the ground far below and the maidens are released from their spell.

As she watched, Rachel became not only Princess Odette, but also Prince Siegfried, the evil magician Rothbart, his daughter Odile, the hunters, and the fluttering swans— jumping, turning, swirling.

Oh, how she danced. And wept.

Rachel began to cry softly when the ballet began and Prince Siegfried meets Odette who, posing in arabesque, softly bends her cheek against her shoulder in a gesture reminiscent of a swan smoothing its feathers. She cried throughout the entire performance, unable to stop, yet she felt happier than she'd ever been before. Papa held her hand, and gave her his handkerchief with the comforting whiff of camphor.

In the closing scene of the ballet, the stage darkens, the music softens, the swan maidens form two diagonal lines at the right. As the light of day gradually rises, their figures are bent low to the ground, in grief at the loss of their queen and in gratitude for their own liberation from the cruel sorcerer. Then on the waters of the lake, a jeweled bark glides into view. Odette and Siegfried, clasped in each others' arms, move in the magical boat to a new and perpetually happy life. The swan maidens raise their heads, their arms fluttering softly like ripples in the water in quiet farewell to their queen.

And the curtain falls.

There was a moment of silence, and then the sound of tumultuous applause, the audience rising to its feet shouting, "Bravo! Bravo!" Papa, usually so quiet and reserved, clapped and shouted along with them. The conductor bowed, then motioned to the musicians to rise. The curtain rose and fell again and again as the dancers took their bows, the audience unwilling to let them go.

It was over. Papa stood up, but Rachel sat for a moment longer in the red velvet seat, clutching the program she wanted to save forever. And right then she promised herself that somehow, some way, she would make her dancing dream come true.

CHAPTER TWO

Back home in the apartment, curled up in the dark beside the sleeping Bronna, Rachel went over the evening performance again and again. She was determined to be a ballerina like those on the stage. Dancing, dancing, dancing. She felt it in her blood, in every breath she took. Finally she fell asleep, a swan floating off into a dream.

The next morning, the same old question plagued her. How was she going to become a dancer without lessons?

Although Mama occasionally said, "You have a gift for dancing, just like Hyman's got a talent to draw," she also added, "We can't afford lessons for anybody. We can barely manage to put food on the table with what Papa earns as an expressman."

Mama didn't wake Rachel up until the last minute. Hyman and Bronna were almost finished eating when she joined them at the breakfast table.

"How was the ballet?" they asked. "Tell us about it."

"Beautiful," she murmured, stretching out the word, her eyelids half-shut, a dreamy smile on her lips.

Before she could continue, Mama admonished, "No talking while you're eating."

Lost in thought, Rachel blew at the hot oatmeal Mama insisted upon making each morning. What good was her talent if she could not fulfill its promise? Other kids were content to get together, play games after school. But she couldn't wait to get home, put her record in the Victrola, and dance.

Once she had asked Papa, "Why am I so different?"

She never forgot his answer. He had grown so solemn and said, "You're not different, you want different things out of life."

Mama's voice burst into her reverie. "Rachel, stop dreaming. Grow up. Finish your porridge."

Rachel gave a pleading look. Sometimes her mother let her get away with just a few bites of her detested oatmeal. But today, Mama's eyes were steely. Rachel remembered how hard the dancers worked last night, how strenuous the routines were. If she wanted to be like them she had to be strong. She quickly finished her oatmeal.

As the children left for school, Mama's voice echoed down the hallway stairs, "It's a sin to waste food."

Humph, thought Rachel, that's one thing her mother never did. She was so frugal. Busy serving her family, the last one to sit down at the table, Mama ate the leftovers, despite Papa's protests.

At school, Rachel was the celebrity of her sixth grade class. The girl who sat in front of her kept turning around whispering questions. "What exactly is a ballet? Is it anything like a stage show? I saw a stage show once. But not at night."

"Ballet is like a stage show but there is no singing—just dancing to the most beautiful music to express feelings," Rachel explained.

"I thought you were poor," the girl remarked.

"We are," Rachel replied. "It was an extra special treat for my birthday."

During recess a few other classmates made a fuss over her, even Betsy and Blanche, the two B's, as she called them. They were best friends and always together. Betsy was acknowledged by all as Teacher's Pet. She was always called upon to erase the chalkboard and when she did, her shining brown curls bobbled like yo-yos up and down her back. Everyone knew her parents changed her name from Bessie Piplakowsky to Betsy Piper. She wore the prettiest dresses, stiffly starched, with matching hair bows. Rachel, with her faded cotton dresses and short, straight, brown hair, felt uncomfortable in her presence.

"I heard *you* went to the ballet," Betsy said in her high-pitched, elocution-school voice. She looked Rachel up and down, and with a toss of her head added, "I can't believe it. Did you?"

"W-why, y-yes," stuttered Rachel, intimidated by Betsy's superior attitude which made her feel like a baby. She felt a hot flush rising on her face.

Blanche gave Rachel a big smile as she said, "Betsy, you're jealous. You wish you could have gone."

"Jealous? Me jealous of Rachel? Don't be ridiculous," said Betsy.

That *was* ridiculous, thought Rachel. But she felt better, and with Blanche so close she took a good look at her. With her fair skin and blue eyes she was like a pretty doll, the golden curls escaping from her woolen cap a shining bright yellow in the sun. The kids in class hinted that her hair was bleached. Sometimes her lips had a purplish glow, which meant she might be wearing lipstick, strictly forbidden in school. Rachel admired her from afar. Blanche went to dancing school.

"How was the dancing?" Blanche asked.

"Wonderful—magical."

"Can I see the ballet program?"

Thrilled at being singled out by her, Rachel offered Blanche the precious booklet.

Holding it close to her pale, almost colorless blue eyes, Blanche said, "It's such small print." As she returned the program she added, "I can't read without my glasses. I hate to wear them at recess."

"Afraid the boys will see you in them?" her friend Betsy teased.

"They're so thick and ugly," Blanche admitted.

Blanche had formerly seemed unapproachable. But now Rachel dared to ask the burning question she never had the nerve to ask before.

"I heard you take dancing lessons. Are they, uh, very expensive?"

"I don't really know. My mother takes care of that." Protectively covering her bangs she added, "My, it's so windy out here, my hair's getting ruined."

Rachel, nervous but determined, persisted. "Could you find out how much the lessons cost?"

"Guess I could ask my mother. I take private lessons with Miss Kelly. She's way out in West Philadelphia."

"Maybe I could go with you sometime," said Rachel, emboldened by a flare of hope. She already pictured herself scrubbing Miss Kelly's studio floor in order to pay for lessons. "Does she give ballet for beginners?"

"Oh, no," Blanche shook her head emphatically. "She only gives tap and acrobatics, which is what I take. No ballet."

"Let's go, let's go," said Betsy, locking arms with Blanche and pulling her away. "Let's watch the boys play ball."

Rachel called after their retreating backs. "Do you know any teachers who give ballet lessons? What they charge?"

"I have no idea," said Blanche, giggling with Betsy as they sauntered off in the direction of the older boys' yard.

"They're two of a kind—vain and boy-crazy," said a classmate coming up beside Rachel. "They think they're such hot stuff."

Rachel watched them until they were out of sight. Stuck-up Betsy and lucky Blanche. Blanche must be rich to get private lessons. She and Betsy really *were* hot stuff.

Rachel hoped Benny Kessler wouldn't see them go by. He was in seventh grade and cute. All the girls like him. She didn't think he knew she existed until about a month ago. During recess he had been playing a game of catch with his friend and the ball sailed all the way from the older boys' yard, landing at her feet. She felt herself blush as she picked it up and handed it to Benny, who had come running for it.

"Thanks, Rachel," he said.

Imagine! He knew her name. Ever since, whenever she saw him, she got the strangest, craziest feelings. Her face got hot, her teeth got cold. Even now she felt that way at the mere thought of him. Someday when she was a famous ballerina he would come to her and confess his love, just like in the movies. Till then, it was enough just to look at him, know he was there.

Right now, getting dancing lessons was the most important thing in her life.

After public school let out in the afternoon, Rachel went to Hebrew school. Before going into class, she stopped a moment to look at the tree on the sidewalk curb outside the school. It was the only one on the block. Sometimes she felt it was lonely and waited patiently to be noticed. A blast of frosty wind rattled its bare branches, then swirled coldly around her. She ran inside.

Getting to bed so late last night and up so early for school, she felt tired and sleepy during class. The teacher's droning voice was hypnotic. With all her might, she willed her eyes to stay open. Otherwise Mr. Julius's ruler would thump between her shoulder blades—the punishment reserved for inattentive students.

But when Mr. Julius asked, "What holiday do we celebrate next month?" her hand was the first to shoot up.

"We have Purim in March," she said.

"Very good, Rachel." The teacher nodded approvingly.

Rachel was proud she knew the answer. Only last night, Mama told them not to touch the prunes and poppy seeds on the pantry shelf. They were filling for the *hamantashen*, the three-cornered pastry she was going to bake for Purim.

As Mr. Julius explained the holiday, Rachel listened avidly, now wide awake. She loved the story about beautiful Queen Esther. How her uncle, Mordecai, the court Jew, intervened with her husband, King Ahasuerus. Together, Queen Esther and Mordecai saved the Jewish people from destruction by Haman, the evil vizier. And to think it all happened more than two thousand years ago in Persia.

It was fun going to synagogue on Purim. The children dressed up in colorful costumes and acted in plays which recreated the ancient story. When the scroll of Esther was read, they loudly booed and jeered at every mention of Haman's name, spinning noisemakers around and around.

Perhaps someday a choreographer would create a famous ballet about Purim. Rachel, of course, would dance the prima ballerina role of Queen Esther.

Later, in the kitchen, she danced in her favorite spot in front of the mirror. Her mother's voice pierced the music. "Always with the dancing. Turn off the Victrola. It's time to set the table for supper."

"Ah, Mama, just another five minutes?"

"It's enough already. I've got a headache from you with the dancing. Papa will be home soon. Let's get ready!"

"Three minutes?"

"A good, religious, Jewish girl doesn't have her mind on dancing."

"Two minutes?"

Mama glared.

With a reluctant sigh, Rachel obeyed.

CHAPTER THREE

The quiet in the kitchen rested on Rachel's shoulders like a comfortable well-worn sweater as she and her family sat around the table after supper. Luckily, she'd found time to dance after helping Mama clean up and put the dishes away. Now she, Hyman, and Bronna were busy with their homework, while her father read the Yiddish paper and relaxed, his long legs sprawled out under the table. The only sound to break the silence was his inhaling and exhaling as he puffed away on a cigarette.

Bronna, fingers threading through her thick blonde hair, pushed her notebook away, sighing, "It's not fair for Miss Bradley to give the fourth grade so much work."

"Look how much Hyman and I have," cried Rachel, "and we're not complaining."

"You should have more—you're older," said Bronna.

"Not that much," Rachel answered quickly.

"I'm only nine. It's too much homework."

"Need any help, Bronna?" Hyman pushed up his horn-rimmed glasses, his light blue eyes, the same color as Mama's and Bronna's, showing concern.

"*Aich bin mut*," Bronna pouted, looking at her mother with a sure-to-win-her-heart beseeching gaze.

"*Nu*, so you're tired—you should still speak English. Papa and I speak Yiddish to you children so you'll know it, but we want you to speak to us in English to help us learn the language better." Getting up to feel Bronna's forehead,

Mama asked, "What's the matter—don't you feel well? Let me see your tongue."

Rachel saw Bronna stick out what appeared to be a perfectly healthy pink tongue. "What's going on here, Ma?" she asked. "What's all the fuss? When I wanted five more minutes to dance before supper you wouldn't let me. But if Bronna says she's tired and doesn't want to do her homework, it's okay?"

"You're older. I expect more from you. And dancing doesn't compare with homework. It's not as important."

"It's…it's important…to me…" Rachel couldn't continue for the hot rush of tears.

Before her mother had a chance to respond, her father spoke softly. "Dora, let me handle this." Then he said firmly, "You must finish your homework, Bronna."

That was that. Rachel should have known that even though Bronna was the baby of the family and twirled everyone around her finger, she would not get out of doing her homework. Not when Papa was around.

"You children are lucky," her father began the refrain they heard so many times. "Here in America, everybody gets an education. I never had a chance to go to school in Russia. You're going to public school and Hebrew school. Be glad you have the opportunity to study and make something of your life."

Though Papa went back to his cigarette as Bronna obediently picked up her notebook, Mama continued the lecture. "How you make your bed, that's how you'll lie in it. You see how hard Papa has to work because he never learned a trade, never went to school. Be grateful *you* can go—so that you can reach out for whatever you want to be."

All was quiet again. The words swam in Rachel's book in front of her. It would be no use to ask—what about *dance lessons*? They didn't give them in school. Even Hyman, who was such a good artist, needed special training. But her parents couldn't afford it. So how could they reach for what they wanted?

It was all so hopeless. With heavy heart she tried to concentrate on her homework.

When they finished, Rachel, Hyman, and Bronna clustered around Papa as Mama puttered in the kitchen. Hyman showed his latest work of art, Bronna sang "My Blue Heaven," and Rachel danced, her depression lifting with each movement of her arms and legs. As Papa extinguished each cigarette, the children took turns taking his Helmar cigarettes out of the silverfoil-lined box for him. And big as they were, all three managed to squeeze onto his lap like a pile of puppies, poking their fingers into the smoke rings he blew for them.

The best part of the evening for Rachel was when Papa tucked Bronna and her under their blanket, and Bronna said, "Tell us a story." Hyman always said he was getting too old for all that, but Rachel wouldn't be surprised if he was listening from his room, because he didn't shut the door. Although she was also getting older—she could almost hear Mama saying, "Grow up, Rachel!"—she still loved to hear the tales, especially with Bronna doing the asking.

"Which story tonight?" Papa asked.

"The Bubbetchka," Bronna quickly replied. "You know, the one where she's a gypsy..."

Though all Rachel could see in the darkness was Papa's silhouette, she knew the smile that would crinkle his lips and she trembled with anticipation. The Bubbetchka's adventures, which had been told to him by his parents when he was a child, were centuries old. As she listened, Rachel felt the presence of her grandparents in the hushed room. Some nights the Bubbetchka was a kindly old lady, other nights a mean witch. Rachel knew the tales by heart, but she hung on each word as Papa drawled, "Once upon a time..." He stopped to take a deep breath. Then with a wondrous rush of words came, "...there was a Bubbetchka."

Rachel sank deeper into her pillow to listen.

"The children were naughty. Although they had been warned by their parents to beware of strangers, they followed the smiling gypsy dressed in trailing scarves of crimson, purple, and gold. Her sweet-playing violin called to them, luring them deeper and deeper into the shadows that filled the forest."

As Rachel listened to Papa telling that familiar story, she heard the violin play, she saw Bubbetchka with all the children in town dancing after her as night fell and the sky blazed with thousands of stars—a ballet enacted in the forest.

Rachel loved these moments listening to Papa's dear, soft voice, and feeling the comfort of his presence in the dark. Too soon, Bronna's little snores meant she was asleep. Too old at eleven to ask her father to continue, she remained silent as he tiptoed out of the room.

She lay awake in the bedroom. She smelled the strong aroma of her father's Turkish cigarette coming from the kitchen. She heard the clink of their nightly glasses of hot tea against the saucers. Her parents probably thought she was asleep because their voices were not lowered.

"The boss doesn't have enough work," Papa said.

Rachel heard her mother's deep sigh. "It's that bad?"

"If I get fired, where will I get another job during these bad times?"

"After you've worked so hard, your boss won't let you go..."

"Hah," Papa interrupted. "Business is business."

"And you've been with him fourteen years," Mama continued. "As long as we've been married."

"He's getting rid of the horse and wagon deliveries. I'm one of the last. You know trucks have taken over. If I had the money, I'd buy a truck and go into the business for myself."

"But you have to know how to read and write English to take the driver's test."

"That's the trouble. With my late hours who has time to go to school or to study at home? Anyhow, how much longer can I carry heavy iron stoves up stairs?"

The shadows flitting around Rachel in the dark drew a picture of Papa carrying a tremendous stove on his back, walking up countless, never-ending flights of stairs, his body slowly shrinking under the load.

Under the blankets Rachel shivered.

Her mother's voice rescued her. "If we could only buy Sam's teahouse. We'd work hard but we'd make a living, you'd be your own boss—what you've always wanted. Maybe we could afford art and dancing lessons for Hyman and Rachel."

How wonderful! Mama discouraged Rachel's dancing, yet she saved for the *Swan Lake* tickets, and now this. A flicker of hope long dormant flared, but only for a moment as she heard Papa say, "Oh, what's the use, Dora. I've talked to Sam for years, offered all our savings. It's not enough. The marvel is you can save at all with the little I give you."

Mama's laugh filtered into the bedrooms. "I don't stint on food—I buy the best. But I know how to shop; nobody can manage the way I do. And none of the children on the block have such healthy red cheeks as ours."

The voices in the kitchen became whispers. The lonely moan of the wind in the desolate night added to Rachel's feeling of hopelessness. If only time hurried by and her dancing dream was fulfilled, she would take care of her parents—they'd never have to worry about money again. She'd buy them a big house, with a garden full of roses...

A shadow appeared, circling around her bed, taunting her: There you go, dreaming again.

She closed her eyes. The little ruffled collar on her flannel nightgown tickled her neck as she cuddled closer to Bronna. Putting her right hand against her heart, as she did every night since she could remember, she began her prayers:

Please God, watch over Mama and Papa. Please find a way for them to get Sam's teahouse so Papa will have his own business and won't have to worry about getting fired. And watch over Bronna...and Hyman... She prayed for everyone in order of importance, and at the last...

...And dear God, please help Mama and Papa buy the teahouse so they'll be able to afford to give me dancing lessons.

CHAPTER FOUR

The next day was Friday, the day Rachel loved best. There was no Hebrew school, and although she ought to rush home to help Mama prepare for the Sabbath, she couldn't resist stopping at the library. She liked its muffled quiet, the high ceilings, and the mountains of books lining the walls, each with its own peculiar, musty smell. On the new books shelf, as if waiting there for her alone, she found a book on dancing. Happily, she signed it out.

After leaving the library, she peeked in the window of the ice cream parlor belonging to Benny Kessler's father, on the corner of their street. Sometimes Benny helped out in the store. There he was, behind the counter by the soda pump, a billowing white apron tied at the waist. He was filling a glass pitcher with seltzer, bubbles fizzing all over the top. She loved catching this furtive glimpse of him and ran home smiling.

The good baking smells of *gefilte* fish and *challah* bread filled the hallway as Rachel rushed up the stairs to their apartment.

"You're late," said Mama.

"I stopped at the library for a few minutes." Rachel threw her coat, school books, and the library book in a heap on the brown leather couch against the wall.

"Get that stuff off the couch. It's for sitting, not for throwing things on."

Ignoring Mama's sharp tone, Rachel grabbed her things, then asked, "Why is it so cold in the kitchen?"

"I like the windows open when I clean. The fresh air purifies for *Shabbos*."

"But, Ma, It's February—freezing outside."

"I just put more coal in the stove. It'll warm up soon."

"So—finally, you're here," Hyman's blue eyes glistened behind his thick glasses.

"We were wondering where you were, Rachel," said Bronna.

"Do you want to see the book I took out of the library?" Rachel asked, holding it up.

Hyman read its title and sniffed. "Ballet dancing is for girls. Whaddaya think I am, a sissy?"

"Come on, Rachel. I'll help you put everything away," little Bronna said. As they entered the bedroom, Bronna leafed through the book. "Oh, what beautiful pictures," she murmured.

Rachel knew her sister's comment was meant to show she understood and shared her love of dancing. She was so sweet. No wonder everyone loved her. Rachel gave her a big hug.

Back in the kitchen, Rachel asked, "Ma, do you have much for me to do?"

"Peel potatoes, help me make the noodles. Why?"

"Can I try out a few new turns?"

"Dancing, dancing, always with the dancing." Mama sighed. "Work comes before pleasure, my girl."

"I'll do the potatoes," Bronna offered.

"No siree. No playing around with knives at your age," said Mama.

"I peeled potatoes when I was nine," Rachel reminded Mama.

"You children don't know how good you have it," Mama said, looking straight at Rachel. "When I think of how I had to help my mother—that's all I'd have to tell her, that I wanted to take time out to dance…"

"Sorry," Rachel interrupted. "Sorry I brought it up." She sat down at the table, ready to peel a big potful of raw potatoes. Mama was cutting vegetables, preparing the salad.

"My mother taught me when I was a *maideleh* that a little girl can't be idle," Mama said. "First thing in the morning, we milked the cow. Then, before the sun rose, we weeded the vegetable garden..."

Rachel glanced at Hyman sitting on the couch. "Now we're in for it," their eyes said as they met. But Rachel didn't really mind. She liked hearing Mama speak about growing up in the small village of Sighet, Hungary, in the shadow of the Carpathian mountains. Rachel looked at Mama's flushed face and tried to picture that child of long ago.

"...I was the oldest," Mama was saying, "busy all day, helping my mother with the cooking, washing dishes, cleaning house, making beds, sewing."

"You were lucky," said Bronna. "You didn't have to go to school."

"Who could go to school? In our poor little *shtetl* only the boys went to the Talmud Torah—the Hebrew school. But my mother came from an Orthodox family and taught me all she knew. She said, 'I don't want you sitting in the syna-gogue looking up at the ceiling while everyone else prays in Hebrew.'"

Mama's bright blue eyes clouded as she continued. "Every year my mother had a baby, twelve in all. Only five lived. I watched her die of a miscarriage with the thirteenth."

Rachel cringed. "How terrible," she said, as though she were hearing it for the first time.

"I was thirteen. I felt so bad, my heart was broken. But I couldn't cry. I could only sigh deeply. My father would say, 'Stop that.' But I never could. It's a habit left with me to this day." Mama sighed the deep, long, drawn-out sigh so familiar to her children—the sigh that took the place of tears. The tears she couldn't shed when at thirteen she found herself motherless.

Mama continued. "I told my father not to worry. I knew how to keep house and could take good care of him and my brothers and sister, which I did. But he soon remarried. Suddenly arrived a stepmother. She resented me and made

22

me miserable. I wanted to go far, far away—America. I worked as a cleaning girl and saved the ship-passage money. Only when I was ready to leave did I tell my father. He begged me to stay.

"'You're too young,' he cried. 'Only seventeen. I don't have much of a dowry for you, but the marriage broker approached me about a *Yeshiva* scholar for you—a decent man—but divorced. You'll stay here and marry him.'

"'I don't want a secondhand husband,' I told my father. 'I'll pick my own. I'm going to America.'"

No matter how many times Rachel heard the tale, her heart filled with pity for Mama. How awful to lose your mother, how sad to have a mean stepmother and a father who didn't understand you. How brave to leave your home and all the familiar faces, and come to a strange country alone. How lucky I am, Rachel realized. I must try not to complain about the chores.

Mama went on, her face brightening, eyes glowing as she told about meeting Papa. "It was love at first sight. I could see the goodness and the kindness in him right from the start.

"He came from Odessa, Russia, and was also without family. He had no trade. He didn't have five cents. But I loved him and we were married. He finally got this steady job as an expressman, delivering stoves and heavy furniture."

Mama told how ecstatic they were when their first child was a son, and they named him Hyman after Papa's mother, Hyka; how Papa would go back and forth a dozen times to look at him in his crib; how he worked harder than ever. Mama's voice grew louder. "If I cautioned Papa not to strain himself doing heavy work, he gathered me and the baby in his arms, murmuring, 'Stones will I carry to make a living for my family.'"

Rachel saw Hyman's dimpled smile as he listened to the tale of himself as a baby.

"When you were born, Rachel," Mama continued, "I was so glad to have a baby girl. I named you Rachel after my

23

mother. And Papa says you look just like his mother, same brown eyes and brown hair…"

Rachel loved to hear about herself. It was as though she was entrusted with the greatest gift of all—to give pleasure to her parents by being a reminder of both their mothers.

"Did they want to be dancers when they were young?" she asked.

"Again with the dancing! In those days, dancing was not a profession for Jewish people."

"But, Mama, from the books I read, the Jewish people have always danced."

"Yes, but only for celebration. It's right there in the Bible that King David danced with all his might before the Ark."

"How about women dancers?"

"Oh, yes," said Mama, nodding her head. "The Bible also tells about Miriam, the Prophetess, dancing with a timbrel in her hand, and all the women followed her with timbrels, dancing as they crossed the Red Sea when it parted for them to escape from Egypt."

"What's a timbrel?" asked Bronna.

"It's a small drum," Mama said. "The rabbis preached perpetual mourning for the destruction of the temple. There was a ban on using musical instruments to accompany dances, so instead they used drums and voices."

Turning to Rachel, she said, "The *Baal Shem Tov*, who founded Hasidism, taught that the rocking motion praying Jews make is a dance to celebrate God. Wherever they were exiled, Jews have always danced to celebrate something, like harvest festivals, holidays, weddings. But not to make their living. You see what I mean?"

Rachel squirmed at Mama's meaning. Nevertheless, she was thrilled the discussion was on dancing and ran into the bedroom, returning with her library book.

"Look, Mama, I wanted to show you this. It says here that in 1463, a Jewish dancing master, Guglielmo Ebreo, wrote the first description of classical dance, and from his manual, ballet was born. See, here's a picture."

Mama, Bronna, and even Hyman gathered to look. Hyman read from the caption. "He taught his rich pupils to 'rise like a little wave.'"

Rachel felt a wave rising within, and lifted her arms to rise with it.

"Someday I'll be the first famous Jewish ballerina," she said.

"Yeah, and someday I'll be the first Jewish president," added Hyman.

"Who's talking about presidents? We're talking about dance," said Rachel. "Tell him, Mama."

Mama's lips pursed in a tight, straight line. She closed the book and handed it to Rachel. "Put it back before it gets dirty, and finish peeling the potatoes. Enough with the dancing."

As Rachel returned the book to the bedroom, she heard Bronna say, "It's not fair. You told the story about Hyman and Rachel, but what about me? Who was I named after?"

Rachel smiled to herself. Bronna was cute. She knew how to get Mama back into a good mood.

Mama was speaking when Rachel came back to the kitchen, her voice low. "Bronna, you're named after my favorite grandmother. Ah, she was a wise one. She taught me to be proud I was a woman."

Mama smiled at Rachel and Bronna as she spoke of her strongly held beliefs. "A woman has the gift of birth, the responsibility to raise her children, to perpetuate the faith, to observe the beauty of the traditions. She is her husband's helpmate." Her mother paused a moment before going into her favorite quote of Solomon's Proverb: "'A woman of worth—who can find her? For her price is above rubies. The heart of her husband trusteth in her.'"

Mama cleared her throat and, reaching across the table took Bronna and Rachel's hands. "If I'm strict, it's only because I try to teach my girls to be women of worth, the way my mother and grandmother taught me."

Hyman burst out, "All this talking about women, women, women. I'm surrounded by them. How come I only have sisters? How come you didn't have more children—I always wanted a brother."

Mama rose up from her chair and threw out her hands, palms up. "A brother, yet! I started to tell you how good you have it compared to when I was a child. Before I know it, I'm writing a book. Rachel can think only of dancing, and now Hyman wants to know why he doesn't have a brother."

"I'll have to be satisfied with sisters." Hyman patted Mama's shoulder. Bronna nuzzled Mama's other shoulder. Rachel wanted to give Mama a hug, too, but at that moment, her mother looked at the clock and frowned.

"Look at the time! Rachel, are you finished with the potatoes? Get me the rolling pin. Bronna—the noodles."

"I'm getting hungry," said Hyman.

"Is that all you have to do? Draw and eat? Go study for your Bar Mitzvah," said Mama. Though she complained, she went to the stove and gingerly extracted a piece of *gefilte* fish from the pot, adding to it some horseradish from the icebox. Hyman blew at the morsel and took a bite.

"Help!" he screeched. "My mouth's on fire."

"You ought to know by now my Hungarian-style horse-radish is hot," said Mama, laughing. "What do you expect? Take a drink of water, you'll be all right."

Mama was queen of the kitchen, tasting the broth, pinch-ing the lettuce to see if it was crisp, snapping orders at Rachel and Bronna to set the Sabbath table. Off came the oilcloth, to be replaced by the linen tablecloth. The freshly-baked *challah* bread, covered by its embroidered *Shabbos* napkin, was placed in the middle of the table. The silver candlesticks that Mama had brought from Europe, her most cherished possessions, were set on each side of it. When Rachel looked at them, she felt the spirit of Bubbe Rachel, her grandmother, joining them.

The children washed, changed clothes, and waited in the kitchen for Papa to arrive. Then together, the family would usher in the Sabbath which, Mama said, made every Jew a king for a day.

"You look so nice for the Sabbath," Mama said, looking them over. "What a shame Papa has to work so late every night. He can't even go to Friday night service with Hyman, and works Saturday so he can't go to morning service with us. In the old country, my father took the boys to Friday night service before sundown while the girls stayed home with mother to prepare. And Saturday, the whole family went to morning service together." She sighed as she went into the bedroom. "Well, I better get dressed."

Soon they heard Papa's unmistakable footsteps coming up the stairs. Before he had a chance to open the door, all three yelled at the same time to Mama, "Papa's home! Papa's home!"

CHAPTER FIVE

"Good *Shabbos*," the children cried in unison as they ran to their father. Rachel permitted Bronna to reach him first. After all, Rachel was older and couldn't act too babyish. Hyman lagged behind, so happy at the sight of Papa he forgot to cover his large front teeth with his fingers as he usually did when he smiled.

I'll bet he'd like to greet Papa the way we used to, Rachel thought, but now it wouldn't look right. Hyman was almost thirteen. And a boy.

When they were younger, they always waited outside for Papa to return from work. Whoever saw him first shouted, "Here comes The Most Beautiful Man in The World." Screaming, they raced to be the first in his arms.

Mama would invariably poke her head out the window to caution, "*Shaah, shaah*," Mama shushed them. "The neighbors will complain."

"Papa's home, Papa's home," they would cry, their happy faces turned up to her.

He was never too tired to lift them, one by one, high to the sky, then down to his cheek for a homecoming, welcoming hug, the clinging smell of tobacco a familiar part of him.

In all the world, Rachel felt she could always depend on Papa's love. Her gentle giant of a father. She remembered asking him repeatedly, "Papa, who's your favorite child? Who do you love best?"

His answer was always the same.

"Such a foolish question," he'd say, smiling. The smile vanished as he lifted his long, slender fingers to his face, palms up, and said softly, seriously, "Look at my ten fingers. I need every one of them. Just as I need and love every one of my three children—all the very same."

It was different with Mama. "I love and treat you three children alike," she proclaimed. Looking threateningly at the strap hanging on the door, she continued, "If any one of you is naughty, you'll get a licking." Strangely enough, even though her threat frightened Rachel, she never remembered getting one.

However, Mama couldn't help showing partiality to blonde, button-nosed, blue-eyed baby Bronna. And to Hyman, who was her one and only son. Her *Kaddish*, the guarantee of a son to say the prayers for her after her death.

Mama depended on Rachel to help with the household chores. Bronna was too young, and it was not proper for Hyman to help with the womanly tasks. Rachel, the one in the middle, felt imposed upon. Between public school, Hebrew school, homework, and housework, she hardly found time to practice dancing. She spent every extra moment in the corner of the kitchen by the mirror, dancing to her favorite record.

Sometimes she caught Mama watching, a strange look on her face. Sometimes her mother would say, "Forget dancing. There's no money for lessons. I don't want you to get hurt dreaming about something that can't happen."

Rachel's hopes sank.

But Papa would say, "If you wish with all your heart, with all your might, somehow you'll make your dream come true."

Papa renewed her hope. And Rachel continued to dance and dream.

Bronna brought Rachel out of her reverie by clapping her hands and asking, "Papa, did you bring anything home for us?"

29

"Here's the Daily News," he said, laying the newspaper on the lounge.

"Move that paper! Why does everybody throw things on the couch?" Mama sighed, as she emerged from the bedroom dressed in a crisply-starched pink cotton dress and apron.

"My, doesn't Mama look pretty?" asked Papa, as Hyman's long arms grabbed the newspaper before Rachel could. "And my children so clean."

"Good *Shabbos*," her mother said. Her tone had changed completely. It was the one she used when Papa made her dimple and smile, a secret smile between the two of them as their eyes met.

Mama does look pretty, Rachel thought, the blue of her eyes lighter than ever against the rosy flush of her cheeks. The fancy tortoise-shell comb she wore for special occasions stood out against the coiled knot of her long, blonde hair.

The tired creases in Papa's cheeks disappeared in his smile. He reached into his slightly bulging pocket.

"What have I here?" he asked.

They all waited expectantly.

"Surprise!" He pulled out a bag with a flourish. "*Halavah*."

"Boy, oh boy," Hyman rejoiced. "Hope it's got nuts."

"For shame, Berel," said Mama, grabbing the bag. "They can't have candy now."

"We won't touch it till after supper," Bronna begged.

"I'll make sure of that," said Mama, in her no-nonsense voice. "Come, children, let Papa wash so we can eat."

A few moments later they took their places at the table. Papa sat at the head, his white shirt shining bright. Mama looked at them approvingly. "Now I can begin."

All eyes were serious while Mama lit the Sabbath candles. She bowed her head, covered with a silk kerchief, and reverently recited the age-old prayer: "*Baruch Atta Adonai Elohenu Melech Ha-o-lam Asher Kid'shanu B'mits-vo-tav v'tsee-va-nu L'had-leek Ner Shel Shabbat.* Blessed art Thou, O Lord Our God, King of the Universe, Who hast hallowed us with Thy Commandments and commanded us to kindle the Sabbath light."

Moving her arms over the candles in a gesture of embrace, Rachel's mother covered her eyes with both hands and prayed for the family. She mentioned everyone—her sister, brothers, and father in Hungary; her brother, Yossel, the cantor in New York; and Papa's brothers in Russia, making Rachel feel like they were all linked at the table. Then Mama spoke her mother's name and the names of other deceased members of the family, invoking them to rest in peace. At this point, every Friday night as long as Rachel remembered, her mother's blue eyes glistened; tears ran down her fingers and shone in the candlelight, almost as if her suffering were part of the prayer. Finally, she sighed deeply and whispered, "Amen, Good *Shabbos*," and kissed them all. The ritual was over.

Rachel's feet danced under the table to the rhythm of the candles' light as it flickered unsteadily and then leapt up in a glowing golden flame. She saw herself as a ballerina in them, the swaying flames a message of hope to her from Bubbe Rachel's silver candlesticks.

Mama was saying, "I remember the Sabbaths of my childhood with my family. I hope when you grow up, this will also be a tender memory for you. As a little bit of musk fills an entire house, so the least influence of Judaism flows all through one's life."

"Why do we light the candles?" asked Bronna.

"Don't they teach you that in Hebrew school?" asked Mama.

Bronna smiled impishly. "You tell it better."

"Well," Mama said. They all could tell she was pleased. "Of the six-hundred and thirteen commandments, there are three special duties for a woman. The rest are for men. To be a good Jewish wife and mother, she must make the Sabbath bread loaf. To 'take *challah*,' as it's called. Before I put the *challah* into the oven to bake, I throw a bit of dough into the fire, saying the ritual prayer. Her second duty is to light the Sabbath candles to welcome *Shabbos* into the home."

"What's the third?" piped Hyman.

"It's an old religious custom. She must purify herself in the ritual bath." Turning to Rachel, she said, "Come, help me serve."

Rachel knew the ritual bath was the purification at the *mikvah*—the cleansing bath which religious women took at the end of their menstrual period. Mama had explained the word "menstrual" to Rachel mysteriously by saying, "It's part of being a woman. When you get a little older, you'll understand." Rachel, sensing her embarrassment, had asked no further questions.

While rising to help Mama, she asked, "Papa, did your mother light the Sabbath candles when you were a little boy in Russia?"

Her father's brown eyes looked sad.

"No," he said. "We were not overly religious."

"Why not?"

"My parents were religious in their hearts. In the city of Odessa, where I came from, they were more concerned with the struggle to make a living."

"What do you mean?"

"We were very poor. My father couldn't afford to send me and my two older brothers to school to study Hebrew. He'd never gone himself and couldn't teach us. But he raised us to be proud of our Jewish heritage—to uphold and believe in it."

"Then you weren't even Bar Mitzvahed?" Hyman asked in surprise.

"No. My mother and father tried to observe the holidays, and teach us the customs as best as they could. We just didn't practice them strictly. They said, 'True religion is not to hurt anyone. To be a good person!'"

Mama spoke up proudly. "The little bit of Hebrew Papa can follow at the synagogue is what I taught him."

"That's right." Papa nodded his head vigorously. "And I'm studying, Hyman, so that when you're Bar Mitzvahed, I'll be able to read my few words at the altar with you."

"See, you children have so much to be grateful for here in America, things you take for granted," said Mama. "That's why, Hyman, I want you to work extra hard with your Bar Mitzvah study. Uncle Yossel, being a cantor, will be able to tell if you make any mistakes."

"We haven't heard from him for a while," said Papa.

"You know him. A year can go by without a word, then suddenly, hut-a-tuh, he's here," Mama replied.

"Hope he comes to Hyman's Bar Mitzvah. Have you written him?" Papa asked.

"Of course. How would it look if he didn't come?" asked Mama. "Who else has he got—the bachelor? Our only relative in this country."

"And a cantor, at that," Papa said proudly.

"With such a golden voice," Mama added reflectively. Stirring herself, she said, "Rachel, take the horseradish," carefully handing her the jar. "Watch the good tablecloth," she cautioned as she laid the heavy platter of pungent *gefilte* fish on the table. "Help yourself, everybody."

"Watch that horseradish, Papa," said Hyman. "I had it earlier."

Everyone watched Papa generously slather his fish with the ivory paste. He took a large bite. His face slowly grew redder and redder. He swallowed. "Dora, this time you outdid yourself. Plenty of pepper in the fish and the horse-radish burning hot."

Rachel, Hyman, and Bronna laughed with Mama as she said, "That's the Russian stomach for you. It can take it."

Papa blew Mama a kiss. "Delicious," he decreed. "Just like my mother used to make."

Mama bowed her head. "That's the highest compliment of all," she said, beaming.

Rachel helped her mother serve the tasty, tender chicken, boiled potatoes, lima beans, the *tzimmis* of cooked prunes and fruit, followed by chicken-noodle soup. And finally, the dessert, homemade sponge cake, served with hot tea and lemon.

"Very good, Dora." Papa's approval brought a smile to Mama's flushed face.

"You won't be wanting the *halavah* now, children, will you?" she teased.

"I ate too much," groaned Hyman.

"Me, too," moaned Bronna.

Mama always cooked enough food on Friday to last for the next few days. No work was to be done on the Sabbath, and since she prepared such an abundance, there was enough food for Sunday, also.

The table had to be cleared, dishes washed, kitchen straightened. Rachel worked at her mother's side, the way Mama had said she worked at her mother's side.

Rachel had often wondered what Mama's mother, Bubbe Rachel, looked like. Maybe she felt close to her because she was named for her. Perhaps that Rachel of long ago had also wanted to dance when she was a child, but because of her way of life it was impossible, and no one ever knew her secret. She was not going to let that happen to her. She would dance for Bubbe Rachel and herself.

She stood, heels together, both feet turned out to form a single line, and stretched her leg out from the hip, practicing ballet's first position. Not a moment of time would be wasted. She was eleven, getting older every day, but somehow she would take dance lessons.

"Rachel, what am I going to do with you?" Mama's voice burst into her thoughts.

"Why? What?"

"I've asked you twice to bring me the platter of leftover chicken to put in the icebox. And there you are, foot in the air, head in the clouds, dancing." She turned to Papa saying, "That's what I mean. All she wants to do is dance."

"That's our little ballerina," said Papa, his eyes twinkling.

As Rachel hurriedly brought her the platter, Mama shook her head slowly from side to side.

By the time Rachel got to bed, she was too tired to listen to the buzzing of Mama's and Papa's voices floating from the kitchen. She lay quietly, staring at the black sky framed by the window. What, she wondered, was out there beyond the darkness? Her eyes made out the curve of a tree branch. Squinting at it, she allowed her imagination to cover a branch with feathers and picture it as a swan, bringing a message of hope to her. Perhaps her prayers would be answered. Perhaps her parents would, somehow, find the money for Sam's teahouse and her dancing lessons. The branch looked more like a swan than ever.

Chapter Six

Saturday morning Papa left early as always, and Rachel, with Mama, Hyman, and Bronna went to morning service at the synagogue so conveniently located a few doors away. Funny, even though she went there everyday after public school, the Talmud Torah looked different today. It smelled different. With the Sabbath glow, you didn't notice how old and in need of paint everything was. Even the teachers didn't look as stern as they did during class. They smiled in greeting to everyone.

Hyman took his seat downstairs with the men. Rachel, Mama, and Bronna sat upstairs in the women's section. Rachel saw Hyman look up at them. When their eyes met, he winked at her.

A warm feeling flooded Rachel. How good it was to be here with her little family, chanting the hymns and singing along with the rabbi and cantor. The lights and candles burning at the altar swam in a blur before her eyes, blending with the picture of Mama lighting the Sabbath candles last night. She saw herself again in the flames, dancing, twirling, swaying. Benny Kessler's face, gazing at her in adoration, was there, too.

Papa got home earlier for supper on Saturday. "Everything on the table will be the same as yesterday, only cold," said Mama, filling their glasses with seltzer from the siphon bottle on the table. Rachel liked to listen to the loud hissing *prrss, prrss* sound of the seltzer spurting.

"I like the chicken better when it's hot," said Hyman.

"You know we're not allowed to light a fire to cook with on Saturday," said Mama.

"What if we did?" asked the ever-curious Bronna.

"It's a sin."

"Gosh, why does everything have to be so scary? You get a sin if you cook, write, or draw on Saturday. You can't do anything."

"Because Sabbath is a day of rest and relaxation. God worked and made the world in six days. On the seventh, He said one should rest, enjoy the home, family and friends, synagogue."

"How were the services today?" asked Papa.

"Oh, they were beautiful," said Mama.

"Wish I could go with my family, but I have to work."

"Mama, will Papa get a sin because he works on Sabbath?" asked Bronna.

"It's different if you must work," said Mama.

"I don't understand, he's still breaking the law."

"He's allowed."

"Why?"

"Because in America, it's hard to be a Jew."

"That's something I've wondered about," said Rachel. "Is it hard to be a Jew in America because our Sabbath is on Saturday and all the stores are open so everybody has to go to work? But the Christians' Sabbath is on Sunday when everything's closed. So they have no problem about working on their Sabbath, and it's easier for them to be observant. It's not fair. How come the Jewish Sabbath is Saturday and the Christian, Sunday?"

Papa busied himself eating. He didn't say a word. But Rachel noticed that mischievous gleam in his eyes as he inclined his head toward Mama for her answer.

"How am I supposed to know about their Sabbath?" Mama cried. "Ask your teacher."

"I know why," volunteered Hyman. "We just learned the other day at Hebrew school that the reason the Christian Sabbath is on a Sunday is because they believe Jesus Christ was resurrected on that day."

"What does resurrected mean?" Bronna asked.

Mama hurriedly thrust a glass of seltzer toward her. "Bronna, drink," she said. "Enough about Jesus!"

"It tickles," Bronna said, sipping the bubbles on the rim of the glass.

"Can I have some more seltzer?" Hyman asked. "I put too much horseradish on my *gefilte* fish again."

"Take some *challah*," said Mama, cutting him a piece of bread and refilling his glass. *Prrss, prrss.*

Rachel asked, "Mama, if you try to be good, not make any sins, would you get rewarded by having your wish come true?"

"It doesn't work that way. You're not supposed to bargain with God or ask for things for yourself. He will decide what's best for you."

When? Rachel thought. How much longer would she have to wait for God to decide about dancing lessons? Her fork, heaped with chicken, now seemed too heavy to lift to her mouth.

"Rachel," Papa said softly. His eyes were serious although his lips smiled. "Remember what I tell you. With God's help, if you want something badly enough, hard enough, *you* will find a way to make your wish come true."

Suddenly her fork felt lighter. She even had seconds of the lima beans. She loved them cold, especially when she mashed them.

"Guess what's for dessert tonight?" Mama asked. She produced a small plate with the three slices of *halavah* Papa had bought last night. The children pounced on them.

Rachel whistled. "Aren't we lucky?"

Mama shook her finger at her. "It's not ladylike to whistle."

"When Mama hides anything, no matter how hard we look we can't find it," Hyman confided to Papa as he gingerly licked, then bit into the *halavah*.

"That's right," Mama agreed proudly. "Anyway, sweets are bad for the teeth."

"Well, it's good for them once in a while," was Papa's defense.

"Mmm, plenty of nuts," Hyman murmured, eyes closed as he chewed blissfully.

"Ya wanna bite?" Bronna offered Papa.

"No thanks, Bronnela," he said, sipping his tea.

"You, Mama?"

"I'm fat enough without *halavah*."

Papa was enjoying his after-supper cigarette, inhaling deeply, then blowing out wreaths of smoke. Rachel got to him before Bronna to stick her fingers into the smoke rings circling around him. One settled right on top of the bald spot on his head and her finger fit right into it.

"Everyone hurry up—finish," said Mama, looking up at the cuckoo clock on the wall. "Papa's having a card game tonight."

Rachel's interest in the smoke rings disappeared. "Oh, you're having a game?"

"Yes, help me clean up. The men will be here soon."

Bronna slid off Papa's lap and went for the broom. "I'll sweep. I like to do that."

With dragging feet, Rachel brought the rest of the dishes to the sink. "Gee, Mama, I hate when they come here to play cards."

"I don't like it either, Rachel. But it's the only way we can make some extra money. They're Papa's friends and they give us a share of the winnings if we let them meet here."

Mama started washing dishes, applying kosher soap to each one and rinsing carefully. Rachel dried and put them away, having grown tall enough in just the past few weeks to reach the cupboard without having to stand on the stool.

They worked in silence until Mama sighed and said, "On Papa's wages, I can't save much."

"I know," Rachel said.

Although Mama explained many times that the occasional card game played in the kitchen was a means to save money, Rachel couldn't get used to the idea being a secret.

They weren't allowed to tell anyone, not even widowed Mrs. Bomerantz, Mama's best friend and confidante.

Gambling. Mama had never used the word and Rachel hated to say it, even to herself. But that's what it was. What if someone found out? What would happen? She shook her head several times to oust the troubling thought. After all, she reassured herself, they'd been having the games for years and had been lucky so far.

Promptly at nine, four men, red-faced from the cold night air, marched in. Papa had known them since he was a child in Odessa.

"*Shalom, Shalom*," they beamed. "Hello, hello."

Rachel marveled at Mama's smiling response to them. Only a moment before, she'd said to Papa, "That's the kind of friends you have. Card players. They like to play games on Saturday night—instead of staying home where they belong."

Papa put the hats and coats in the hall closet, while Mama led the way to the chairs around the kitchen table. Hyman, Bronna, and Rachel stood lined up for friendly inspection.

Maxie, the short one, said wistfully, "Each time I come here, your children seem to grow another inch."

"They'll be as tall as their parents," commented Dreyfus, settling his big, husky body comfortably on the kitchen chair.

Dave, the third man, was extremely thin. Rachel was always fascinated by his bony Adam's apple that bobbed up and down in his neck. He said, "They get better looking every time I see them."

"*Kinnehurra*," Mama said quickly. Then she added, "Not that I believe in the evil eye, but I say it anyway after a compliment. It's hard to give up the old country's superstitions."

The last of the foursome was called Reds, obviously because of his full head of flame-colored hair. "Here's something for you because you're good kids," he said, showing them a shiny nickel.

"No, thank you," Rachel managed, giving a pleading look to Mama, who never wanted her children to accept money without her permission.

"Take it, take it," Reds insisted.

Mama slowly nodded. Bronna and Hyman quickly took the money. Then Rachel. They all politely murmured, "Thank you."

Papa managed to hug them simultaneously. "I may not have wealth, but I have three wonderful children," he said. "Hyman, show the men your drawings."

Hyman disappeared into the bedroom to get them. Dave took a pear from the bowl of fresh fruit Mama had set on the table. "I hear Sam's teahouse is for sale," he said.

The nickel felt hot in Rachel's palm, which suddenly began to sweat.

Papa said, "I know. He's been wanting to sell for years, but who can afford his price?"

"I hear he's sick," said Dave.

"Yeah." Dreyfus lit the fat cigar he was never without, ignoring Mama's fingers held to her nose wrinkled in distaste. Along with the grey smoke came the words, "I hear he's sick of working so hard."

Reds grabbed a piece of apple strudel Mama offered. "With your marvelous cooking, Dora, and ..." he paused to smile fondly at Papa, "everybody loves you, Berel, it would be a perfect business for you two. It's a shame you can't buy it."

Papa shrugged his shoulders with resignation. But Rachel read in his crooked smile a gleam of hope that he hadn't given up altogether on his dream. She remembered what he said at the dinner table. "If you want something badly enough, strongly enough, you'll find a way to make that wish come true." The card game was a way for him to try.

"Times are so bad, where's the prosperity President Roosevelt said was right around the corner?" asked Maxie.

"It's not on my pushcart corner," shrugged Dreyfus.

"Don'tcha think he's come up with a whole lot of good programs in his New Deal?" asked Dave.

Before anyone could respond, Hyman shyly presented his most recent sketches. One was of the four of them at the table, playing cards, which was met with delightful approval. As they admired the rest, Hyman smiled broadly, deep dimples going chiseled in his cheeks. For the millionth time, Rachel wished that she had inherited Mama's dimples instead of him. They really lit up a face enchantingly. It was certainly more important for her or Bronna to have them because they were girls. Then again, they were lucky they weren't nearsighted like him and in need of glasses. When all was said and done, she was better off without dimples if the near-sightedness had to come with it. How could she possibly dance with those thick glasses? Watching Hyman peering closely at his drawings, her heart melted with sympathy for him, dimples and all.

"Bronna," Papa called. "Sing a song and make with the motions—the way I like."

"I don't feel like it," Bronna whined.

"Come on," Mama commanded.

"No." Bronna gave a childish stamp of her foot.

"Sing, sing, don't be bashful," the men joined in, entreatingly.

Bronna ran into the bedroom, Papa fast behind her.

It puzzled Rachel that Bronna, who was so friendly and outgoing otherwise, always had to be coaxed to sing. Rachel couldn't wait to be called. Unabashed, she said, "While Papa's trying to get Bronna out, shall I dance?"

"Later Rachel," Mama said. "Help us get Bronna to sing."

The whole family begged and pleaded. Bronna reluctantly returned to the kitchen. A moment later, blue eyes sparkling, blonde curls shaking, smiling and gesturing, she sang, "Just Mollie and me, and baby makes three, we're happy in my blue heaven."

Above her voice, Papa prompted delightedly, "Make with the motions!"

"She'll be a singer or an actress someday," one of the men commented. Mama and Papa glowed.

Rachel saw Dreyfus shift in his chair uncomfortably.

"It's my turn," she said, going to the phonograph to put on her record, *Swan Lake*, and perform.

"You're all very talented children, and I'd like to see you dance again, Rachel. But it's time to get on with the game, already," said Dreyfus, reaching for the deck of cards. "It's getting late."

"Deal," ordered Dave. Maxie and Reds held their hands out for their cards.

Papa looked at the men getting ready to play, then at Rachel. Giving her hand a squeeze, he said softly, "You'll be the first to entertain the next time they come. The game is starting, children. Go to bed."

Bronna and Hyman obeyed, but Rachel stood rooted on the spot. "But I didn't get my turn." She tried to stop her lower lip from trembling as the words slipped out between the edge of her tears. "What about me?"

"Children should be seen and not heard," Mama reproved, forcibly ushering Rachel out of the kitchen. Too hurt to cry or even say another word, Rachel threw her nickel as far away as she could. Then she sat rocking dully on her small rocker. It was quiet. Bronna, in bed, didn't say a word.

Rachel finally slid in beside her. "Don't feel bad," Bronna whispered, touching Rachel's arm. That warm gesture released her tears.

"Don't cry," Bronna pleaded, gently patting her sister. Rachel's tears came faster, like a pent-up storm breaking. Bronna continued, "They were mean. They could have waited a few minutes for you to dance."

"You didn't even want to sing, yet Mama and Papa begged you. And I don't blame them. You're the youngest, and you are cute. And Hyman's the boy, the oldest and the artist...they love to show him off. But me, I'm always the unimportant, middle one." A new wave of tears overflowed.

"Ahhh. You know Mama and Papa love you."

"Funny way of showing it."

"They couldn't help it. It was that fat Dreyfus's fault."

Rachel was starting to feel better after her cry. She remembered the way Papa squeezed her hand. He meant to show her he understood. And how about Papa taking her to the ballet, Mama saving for the tickets? Being singled out like that for a special birthday treat—something they never did for Bronna or Hyman.

Wiping her face on the pillow she blurted, "I guess so."

"Someday you'll be a big ballerina and show them all."

"If I ever get dancing lessons," agreed Rachel, thinking how nice Bronna was. Soon Rachel was talking freely and Bronna's answers were coming slower and slower until they stopped in the middle of a sentence. She was asleep.

Rachel got out of bed to look for the nickel she'd flung on the floor. When she found it, she hid it in her drawer, and climbed back into bed. She heard the muffled voices of the men. Despite the secrecy of the game, occasionally they raised their voices excitedly. Rachel heard Mama warn, "*Shaah*, if the neighbors hear, they'll squeal on us."

Rachel grabbed her pillow and hugged it tightly. The card players' voices grew louder. As the rumbling persisted, she jumped out of bed and opened the door slightly to peek into the kitchen. Mama was waving her hands wildly, cautioning the men, "Be quiet! You want trouble? It's late. Everyone's asleep in the building. You want to wake them up and give us trouble?"

Dreyfus ignored her, screeching, "What kind of pinochle players are you? You don't know how to play the game!"

"Don't give lessons," Dave snapped. "You're mad because you're losing."

"C'mon, Dreyfus, pay up!" shouted Maxie.

As Reds opened his mouth to join in, there was a loud knock at the door. Everyone fell silent.

The knocking grew more insistent, but Mama and the men were stock-still.

Panicking, Rachel hugged herself tightly. This was it, her worst fears realized. Someone had reported them and now the police were coming to drag Mama and Papa off to jail. Tomorrow all the kids in school would find out. Even Benny Kessler!

Mama put a finger to her lips to signal silence from the men as she opened the door.

Rachel held her breath.

Little Mrs. Bomerantz, their neighbor, stood in the door. "Forgive me, Dora, if I frightened you," she said. She slipped inside the apartment and closed the door softly behind her. "Though you never told me about these games, I've known about them all along. I'm not a good sleeper as it is, so when they come, I keep watch. After all, I'm your best friend. But tonight," Mrs. Bomerantz shook her head sorrowfully. "Tonight was *murder!*"

Mama sighed deeply and hugged her in silent gratitude.

Mrs. Bomerantz patted Mama's back and turned to leave. "So keep it quiet, boys," she added, pointing a warning finger at the card players.

"Ohhh," Rachel breathed with relief as she crept back to bed. Bronna was sleeping soundly beside her, and Rachel marveled that Papa and Hyman had also slept through the commotion. She said her nightly prayers, including a special thank-you mention for Mrs. Bomerantz, their self-appointed protector, and then she fell asleep.

The stale smell of tobacco woke her early the next morning. The men were finally gone, but the ordinarily spotless kitchen was in shambles. Ash trays containing dozens of cigarette and cigar stubs were everywhere. All was quiet. Papa, Hyman, and Bronna were still asleep. Mama was in the kitchen opening the windows wide, letting in the cold, fresh air.

"What are you doing up so early?" was her greeting.

"I couldn't sleep anymore."

Blue eyes narrowing, Mama scrutinized Rachel keenly. "You all right?"

Rachel nodded.

Mama looked at the window. Patches of early morning fog had left a cloudy breath on the window panes. "It looks like snow," she said.

Rachel went to her side to help clean up, saying a silent prayer of thanks they hadn't been caught—this time.

Would they ever have enough money to buy Sam's tea-house and end the card games?

CHAPTER SEVEN

Papa left early Sunday morning—an unusual occurrence. That was the one day in the week he got up late and had breakfast with the family. Mama made herring and potatoes for Sunday breakfast, but the children still had to have their bowl of oatmeal.

"Just a small one today. It's so good for you," she said.

Bronna looked up from her bowl and asked, "Did you hear about Blanche Ross?"

Rachel sat up, alert. Blanche of the yellow hair and shining lips—the only girl she knew who was lucky enough to take dancing lessons. "No, what?"

"I saw her younger sister, Toby, at services yesterday," Bronna blew on her oatmeal and took a spoonful. "She told me it happened Friday."

"Told you what?" Rachel rapped on the table in exasperation.

"Well, she was having a race, running with some boys and girls after school..."

"That Blanche and her girlfriend, Betsy, are always running—running after the boys," interrupted Hyman.

"Go *on*, Bronna," urged Rachel.

"Toby says Blanche is blind without her glasses but she's so vain, she hates to wear them. She had a bad bump into a pole and fell. They had to take her to the doctor."

"Oh my gosh—how is she?"

"She broke her ankle. She's on crutches."

"No! How awful!" gasped Rachel. "I can't believe it."

"It's a shame," nodded Bronna.

"Why didn't you tell me about this when you heard? You know she's in my room in school."

"I forgot. I just remembered."

"How do you know so much about her? She's new in my class. I didn't even know she had a sister."

"They moved next door to my girlfriend, Fannie, around the corner. They became friends and that's how I met her," explained Bronna.

"Is Toby pretty like her sister—does she have blonde hair and dance, too?"

"Nah—she wears thick, horn-rimmed glasses, has dark brown hair and is fat. Says she's the ugly duckling."

"Poor Blanche, She won't be able to dance," said Rachel. "She must be heartbroken."

"Nah. Toby says her sister hates dancing school. She only goes because her mother drags her."

Rachel shook her head in disbelief. How strange. Blanche had lessons and didn't want them. Rachel wanted lessons and couldn't get them.

Mama's eyes met her as though she were reading her thoughts. However, all she said, softly, was, "Eat your oatmeal."

"I'm going to my friend's to do homework," said Hyman.

Rachel suddenly remembered his comment about Blanche and her girlfriend, Betsy, running after the boys. Not for a moment had she thought he'd ever noticed girls.

"You better wear an extra sweater under your coat," Mama cautioned. She got up from the table to open a window, thrusting her hand out to test the weather. "It's getting so cold, I don't believe it will snow after all."

After he left, Bronna and Mama took chicken soup to Mrs. Bomerantz, who lived second-floor-back. Rachel was glad to be left alone. She spent the afternoon dancing to her record in front of the mirror, playing it over and over as loudly as possible. Thinking about Blanche on crutches, Rachel stretched her legs with greater fervor than ever.

While dancing she hadn't felt cold, but in the late afternoon, sitting on the leather lounge reading the library book, she felt chilly. She imagined the wind becoming furious, roaring, "Let me in!" and finally slipping through the ill-fitting sash of the tightly-shut windows. It made Rachel nervous.

She was glad when her mother and sister returned. When Mama sat down on the lounge to read the Jewish newspaper, Rachel complained, "It's chilly in here."

"I'll check the stove in a moment," said Mama. "*Oy*, all you read in the paper is about how bad times are—people losing their homes, selling apples on corners, the bread lines. It says here a block-long line of people waited at a bakery to buy day-old bread."

Hyman came in shouting, "Boy, it's really winter out there." Going to the stove to warm up, he shuddered, "And inside, too. The stove's not hot."

Mama rose with a sigh and relinquished her paper. "I guess I'd better fix the fire before it goes out altogether," she said. "It's awful when things are so bad even coal's a luxury."

"Gosh, it's all right if I freeze. But all Hyman has to say is he's cold, and he gets action," Rachel grumbled.

"What kind of word is gosh? And why are you always so jealous?" asked Mama. Dipping her shovel into the coal bucket behind the stove, she opened the door to the stove and shoveled the coal into the feeble fire.

Rachel watched as the weak flame licked the fuel. She decided not to answer Mama, whose face was getting very red as she poked the embers and threw in some more coal.

Hyman, however, started singing, "Rachel, please tell us, why are you jealous?"

Ha! Rachel thought. He has to tease me!

"Ah, let her alone, Hyman," begged Bronna, looking sympathetically at Rachel.

Unable to contain himself, Hyman laughingly continued, "Rachel, please tell us, why are you jealous?"

Rachel was suddenly boiling hot. "Say it one more time—I dare you, and I'll…I'll scratch your stupid face!"

"That's enough, Hyman," yelled Mama, holding up the shovel, glaring at him. Rachel felt much better. Then, pointing the shovel at Rachel, Mama continued, "And I don't want to hear any talk of scratching. Grow up, Rachel. You're not too old for the strap, either of you."

There was silence.

It felt good to hear Mama scold Hyman, even though Rachel was also reprimanded. Mama thought Hyman was so perfect.

I guess I really am jealous, Rachel thought, but I can't help it.

A yellow-red tongue of fire suddenly leaped as though to escape the stove's prison chamber. Mama hurriedly clanged the door shut. "It'll soon be nice and warm," she said, then stopped abruptly, hand to her ear, listening to the footsteps slowly coming up the hallway stairs. They stopped on the second floor.

Rachel knew Papa's footsteps by heart. She could have told Mama right away they weren't her father's.

"Where *is* Papa?" Rachel asked. "He sometimes has an odd job on Sunday, but he's always home by this time."

"Yeah, that's what I'm wondering." Hyman's voice ended on a high, plaintive note as he went to the window.

Bronna joined him. Mama was making hot water for tea and the steam from the kettle misted all the window panes. It was impossible to see through them.

Bronna rubbed off the vapor with her fingers, making a circle to look through. "I don't see him outside," she fretted.

"Here he is," Hyman grinned, as with his index fingers he added a neck and body to the circle Bronna had made on the window. 'I'd better give him a scarf and hat, too," he joked, quickly sketching them in. "It's so cold."

"That's good," said Rachel, smiling at Hyman. He really is a swell artist, she thought proudly. Even if he does tease me.

"All right, children. That's enough drawing," Mama called. "Much as I hate to have supper without Papa, we'd better. Everything's getting dried out."

"No. I want to wait," cried Bronna.

"He probably got tied up with those wonderful friends of his," said Mama. "It's very late."

Hyman said, looking out the window, "Just listen to that wind."

In the moment's silence, the window rattled louder than ever.

Mama said, "It's very late," and Rachel knew from her puckered brow that she was worried. Who could eat now? Papa almost always spent Sundays with them. He would never want to cause them alarm. Something beyond his control must be keeping him. The night had never looked so black. A chill of fear crept down her spine.

"Maybe something's happened to Papa," she said.

Mama gave one of her deep-down sighs. "I guess we could wait supper a few more minutes."

The words were no sooner out of her mouth when they heard the footsteps that could belong to no one else but Papa running up the stairs.

As he opened the door, the look on his face was different from other nights.

"Why so late? Where have you been?" Mama hurled questions at him.

"Dora, Dora, guess what! Sam's going to sell me the teahouse!" The words tumbled out of his mouth like bombshells.

Rachel couldn't remember such a big smile on her father's face. She was astonished to see Mama sink down on the lounge and burst into tears.

"What's the matter?" Bronna asked as they circled around her.

Mama looked at them, smiling and sobbing at the same time, saying, "It's a *mazel tov*. I'm crying because I'm so happy."

Papa squeezed Mama's hand and gave her a rare kiss which landed on the top of her head.

Although Mama said, "Berel, not in front of the children," Rachel could tell she was pleased from the deep dimple in her cheek.

"Just look at you standing there, like a stranger, with your coat and hat still on. Take them off and hurry, tell us all about it," Mama laughed, pointing for him to sit beside her. Everyone joined in the laughter. Papa wriggled out of his coat, which fell into Rachel's waiting arms.

She struggled to hang his coat, heavy and stiff from the cold, in the closet. She felt elated. Was it possible that at last, she might take dance lessons?

Everyone was seated on the lounge. Bronna obligingly moved over to let Rachel squeeze in next to Papa.

"Tell us, already—what happened?" they cried.

"You remember last night at the card game, the men said Sam was sick," said Papa. "I thought I'd go over and see what was what. That's where I've been all day. Sam has to get out of the teahouse—it's too much for him. Looks like I'm the only customer that can take over right away."

"So how is it nobody else wants to buy the teahouse?"

"Who knows? But that's our good luck."

"How much money does he want?"

"Ah, the money." Papa paused, looking grave, then continued. "That's the big thing. I don't have enough to meet his price. But," he added quickly, smiling, "Sam's so anxious to get out, he'll take what I have as a down payment. The rest he'll let me pay out in monthly installment payments over a few years. It'll be a struggle, Dora. I told him I'd have to talk it over with you." He looked at Mama. "What do you say?"

Rachel realized Mama didn't look happy. With her lips tightly compressed, Mama pondered a moment, and then asked, "What'll happen if business is bad and we aren't able to meet our payments? You know there is a Depression going on."

"That's the gamble we have to take."

Another gamble, thought Rachel. The prospect of her dance lessons suddenly grew dim. She waited to hear Mama's response.

The dimple was back in Mama's cheeks. "Anything's better than you *schlepping* those heavy stoves up all those stairs every day, Berel."

Papa looked down at the floor in silence. He swallowed, then said softly, "Thanks, Dora. You're a good wife."

In his voice, Rachel detected a tremor which was most unusual in her six-foot-tall mountain of a father.

Bronna and Hyman besieged Papa with questions.

"When are you taking over the teahouse?"

"Are we going to move?"

"Move? Where to?"

"One at a time," laughed Papa. "Sam and I have a lot of things to straighten out. He needs someone right away. I'll talk to him tomorrow, and give notice to my boss. And yes," he nodded, "we will be moving to rooms over the teahouse."

Rachel felt a lump in her chest. She was digesting the words Papa had used, *struggle* and *gamble*, as they related to her dancing lessons. The teahouse had seemed the only way to get them. She had clung to that hope all along. She still would.

Moving? She hadn't figured on that. She'd lived here all her life. She was accustomed to the worn hallway steps, the faded, flowered wallpaper, the dancing spot by the Victrola in the kitchen. The public school across the street, Talmud Torah a few doors away.

Papa was saying, "Sam's rooms are full of furniture; it's part of the sale. Old, but better than ours."

"That's good," Mama interrupted, "because our furniture is falling apart—except, of course, for the lounge."

Rachel felt a pang for the old, broken, familiar furniture.

"Will we have to switch schools?" Hyman asked.

"I'll find out," said Mama. "We'll be moving about six blocks away so we may be in another public school district. But you can continue with the Talmud Torah here. If you have to transfer, the walk after public school to Hebrew school will do you good."

Rachel pictured herself reporting to a new teacher, in a new school, a new class, with everyone looking her over. She always felt sorry for the new girl appearing in the middle of the term. Now she would be that girl.

And how about Benny Kessler? Though he was unaware of her feelings, he was part of her world. She was content to adore him silently, catch glimpses of him at school or in his father's store. The prospect of possibly not seeing him filled her with desolation.

"Let's eat!" Papa cried as he went to the kitchen sink to scrub his hands. "I'm starving."

Rachel had no appetite whatsoever. She could barely tolerate the aroma of the food, but made a pretense of picking at it. Even her favorite, lima beans, went untouched.

Mama didn't make an issue of it. "Everybody's excited tonight," she said, the dimple flashing more than ever.

"Won't it feel queer to move away?" Rachel asked Hyman and Bronna later.

"Yes." Bronna was unusually solemn. "I'd rather not."

Rachel waited to hear what Hyman would say. He was older, and very smart in school, especially arithmetic, which Rachel hated.

"It's sure gonna be a big change," he said, forehead puckered and blue eyes instantly serious behind his glasses.

The wind died down to a soft whisper and kept time to Bronna's sleepful breathing as Rachel said her prayers:

Thank you, dear God, for helping Mama and Papa get the teahouse. But, I must admit, I'm worried about the dancing lessons. Papa said there's a struggle ahead, and a gamble—that's what we've had all along. I don't want to sound selfish. I know the main thing is Papa won't have to work so hard to make a living and I'm happy about that. But what about my lessons?

Mama says I'm not supposed to ask you for favors, but Papa says with your help and if I try with all my might, I will find a way to make my dream come true. So I'm not asking for a favor, just for help. That somehow they'll be able to squeeze some money from the teahouse for my dancing lessons. That's the only way I can see, right now.

Rachel lay awake long after she finished. Only by summoning the music of *Swan Lake* was she able to escape her thoughts. Just like the ballerinas, in white satin and tulle, high on her toes she danced her way through the shadows—to sleep.

CHAPTER EIGHT

Papa gave his boss two weeks notice. The children saw him only for a few moments late at night, when he was exhausted. Early the next Sunday morning, he was off again.

"Can't you have breakfast with us, Papa?" Rachel asked, as Mama served split fish with onions. "It's your favorite."

"Please, Papa," Bronna begged. "We hardly saw you all week."

The morning sun blazing through the window lit up Hyman's front teeth, magnifying them as he nodded in smiling agreement.

"It doesn't seem right to have Sunday breakfast without you," Mama entreated.

He can't resist all of us, thought Rachel.

"Sorry, but I've got to get to the teahouse. There's so much to do before I take over. And Sam needs me."

"Papa has to leave," said Mama.

Throwing them a kiss on his way out, Papa said, "I love you."

"Me, too," Rachel, her brother, and sister sang in unison.

The tired lines on Papa's face disappeared as he said, "It's going to be a beautiful day. Why don't you all take a walk to the teahouse this afternoon? I'll show you around."

"Remember your manners when we get to the store," Mama cautioned as they hurried along, the brisk wind at their heels. Keeping an eye out for the signs, Rachel called out the name of each street they passed and at the sixth shouted, "Look—the sign says Gaskill Street. We're here."

Although excited at seeing the teahouse at last, her first thought was that it was not a great distance—she could see Benny Kessler at his father's ice cream parlor when they moved. Maybe even go in and get a soda, if she had the nerve.

"There it is! That's the teahouse!" Mama exclaimed as they turned the corner.

"Where? Where?" Rachel and her brother and sister all shouted at once.

Rachel craned her neck to stare down the narrow street. She saw an attractive, modern building with a large store-front window. Her heart fluttered. Could this be it? But Mama pointed elsewhere. "There!" she said. Rachel's heart dropped.

So tightly wedged between the row-houses that if you didn't look quickly you would pass it by, was the teahouse. It was so small! This was the dream Mama and Papa talked about for such a long time? Rachel hadn't known what she'd expected, but in the farthest reaches of her imagination, it was not this hole-in-the-wall.

Her father had been so proud when he told them about the sign he'd had painted on the window: "The New Odessa Teahouse and Restaurant—Kosher." Staring at it, she realized she didn't have the heart to tell him the sign-painter misspelled it as *Odeser*.

The faded, frayed curtain hung limply, as though it would fall apart at the very next touch. Warped and peeling woodwork framed the windows. Several bricks were missing from the red brick front, and a few more were poised as though threatening to fall at any moment.

Hyman met Rachel's eyes. "Kinda beat-up looking, isn't it?" he asked.

She nodded, unable to say anything. She had such a funny, empty feeling in her stomach.

Hyman took Rachel's hand. She knew he understood what she was feeling. "Well, let's see what it's like inside," he said.

As they went in, she saw Papa looking at the door expectantly. His face lit up at the sight of them. He looked so happy, Rachel felt ashamed. The store meant so much to him.

"Come in and meet Sam," Papa said, leading them to the food counter. Rachel's mouth watered at the delicious-looking food in the white refrigerator case.

Treats they had only on Sunday morning were displayed: thick, browned-to-a-crisp pieces of baked herring, oil-bronzed chopped herring, spiced *shmaltz* herring, exotic fish from far Odessa that Papa's Russian taste buds craved and rarely could afford—dried *kupchunka*, butter-soft *bellaribitza*, and *lox.* Rachel salivated at the thought of its strong, salty taste.

She took a deep breath. If she had a choice she didn't know what to choose. Maybe a taste of each on a bagel, with a thick slice of onion.

"My!" She licked her lips. "Doesn't everything look good?"

"It sure does," Hyman said. "But see that dish of brains? Who would want eat them?"

"Ugh," Rachel turned her head to avoid looking at the gray, coiled mass. She noticed Bronna's eyes lingering on the apple strudel heaped on a plate on top of the counter. Suddenly, daredevil Bronna reached out for a piece.

Mama grabbed her hand. "Don't—*mir toornisht!* It's forbidden. Put it back," she said in her wait-until-I-get-you-home-for-not-minding-your-manners voice.

Luckily, Papa hadn't seen or heard. He was talking with Sam, who was standing behind the counter. Rachel knew that Papa was taller than most people, but next to Sam he looked like a giant. Mama always said Papa looked even taller than his six feet because he was so thin. Now, with eyes shining proudly, his voice rang out for all to hear, "This is my family."

Sam said, "Hello..." and stopped to take a deep breath.

All Rachel could think about was how tired he seemed—and old. His hair was almost completely gray, only a trace of brown remaining. The shaggy gray mustache which overlapped his upper lip made Rachel think of a walrus. But he looked sick—for even his face was gray. Well, she reminded herself, he *was* sick. That was why he was selling the teahouse.

Sam was saying, "I see you have some helpers, Berel. You'll have plenty of work for them here." His attempted laugh ended in a wheezing cough which caused the long hair on the ends of his mustache to quiver.

Rachel thought, I'm glad we're all strong and healthy. We'll never let Papa get to be like Sam.

Her father clapped his hands. "Well, now I'll show you around the place."

So much to see all at once! A jumble of mismatched chairs around polished wooden tables, shiny glass spittoons on the worn wooden floor beneath each table. The customers sitting at the tables stared at them. Rachel felt uncomfortable with so many strange faces watching her. She peered sideways to avoid their glances.

"Look," Papa said. "See the samovar!" He pointed to the huge metal urn with steam coming out of the top. It stood on four legs, and had a spigot. Inside, Papa explained, was a tube for heating the water to make tea. Rachel had never seen anything like it.

"It's just like the kind we had in the teahouses back home," he said with pride.

A table next to the samovar held brown pots of two sizes—the larger one for hot water, and the smaller one that fit on top, for tea. Many delicate glasses were lined up on the side, along with a dish for sugar cubes and a dish for lemon slices.

"A real Russian likes his tea brewed in a teapot—boiling hot water from the samovar poured into a glass with a slice of lemon, and a cube of sugar on his tongue. He can drink tea, relax with his friends from his hometown, and have a good Jewish home-cooked meal when he gets hungry."

Papa stretched out his arms to encompass the store's four walls. "It's all waiting for him in our New Odessa Teahouse."

"What are they doing?" Hyman asked, motioning to a table in back of the store where four seated men were in deep concentration playing a game, while several men huddled over them, standing watch.

"I told you this teahouse was like the ones in Odessa," Papa said. "They're playing dominoes, a favorite Russian game."

Rachel recognized the four men from the card game in their kitchen. Reds, with the bright red hair, Dave of the nervously woggling Adam's Apple, Dreyfus, munching away at a cigar, his burly body overlapping the chair, and short Maxie watching on tiptoe. None of them was interested in saying hello at a crucial point of the game. She was relieved that they wouldn't be playing illegal card games in their apartment anymore.

Rachel saw two other men standing behind the domino players, watching the game intently. The man next to Maxie shouted, "Hey, Dave. That was a wrong move!" at which point Maxie jabbed him with his elbow, reprimanding him, "Keep your mouth shut! What are you, a *kibitzer*? You want to get thrown out of here?"

"Okay, okay," the man growled, and shut his mouth.

The last stop was the kitchen, so hot it felt like July. Frank, the dishwasher, nodded, and kept working. Mrs. Cohen, the cook, beamed as they entered. Despite being tremendously overweight and sweating profusely in the hot kitchen, she seemed happy. It must be because of all the good food, Rachel thought, as she savored the tantalizing cooking aromas.

Mrs. Cohen was arranging plump potato knishes, fresh from the oven, on a large platter. Rachel's eyes feasted on them hungrily. Potato knishes were her number one favorite.

"What lovely children you have," laughed Mrs. Cohen. "Can they have a knish?"

And Rachel loved Mrs. Cohen instantly, because she gave *her* the largest one.

In the midst of preparations for the grand move, Mama threw a bombshell. When Rachel came home from school, she couldn't believe her eyes. Mama had a haircut! She looked so different without her thick blonde hair coiled in the familiar knot at the nape of her neck. Rachel shook her head in amazement.

"It will take time for everyone to get used to it, but I like it," Mama said, fingering her cropped hair.

"I do, too," smiled easygoing Bronna.

"But Papa's not going to like it," observed Rachel.

"That's for sure," Hyman nodded wisely.

"I know," Mama agreed. "Do me something, he likes my long hair. I keep telling him this is modern times and I'm the only one on the block with long hair, but he's against me cutting it. Now that he's so busy getting ready for the teahouse, I figured it's a good time to cut it; he may not even notice it."

But when Papa arrived, he noticed it instantly. "Dora! What did you do?"

A flurry of words ensued between them as Papa voiced his disapproval and Mama tried to calm him down. Finally, she pointed out, "This way it will be much more hygienic for cooking in the teahouse kitchen." That did it.

Moving day finally arrived. They took very few possessions in the truck. Sam's furniture, though well-used, was better than theirs. Rachel made sure to take her little wooden rocker, though.

"What do you want to take that old thing for?" Mama cried. "It creaks and the wood keeps getting unglued. Besides, you're getting too big to fit into it."

"Please let me take it," Rachel begged, holding it tightly in her arms.

"Let her have the rocking chair, Dora," Papa urged.

"I hate to drag it with us, but if it means so much to you, all right," Mama grudgingly agreed. "It's time to grow up, Rachel," she added.

Rachel felt very sad about leaving their old neighborhood. Nevertheless, the new living quarters above the store were nicer. In their old apartment, their kitchen also served as a dining room and parlor. Here, the kitchen was next to the store, downstairs. As you came up the stairs to the second floor, there was a bathroom on the right. And to the left, a dining room held an antiquated table, chairs, and a china closet, with a complete set of yellowed doilies on the buffet.

Through the dining room, Rachel walked into the front room. It was the parlor. She gasped. A mirror reached from the top of Mama's precious leather lounge and covered the wall to the ceiling. Though a bit discolored and cracked on its edges, it was the mirror she had always longed for, but never expected to own. Now she could practice dancing to perfection, on her very own stage.

Their phonograph beckoned from its new position in the corner of the room. Like a sleepwalker in a trance, she put on her *Swan Lake* record. As the music played, she danced, watching herself in the mirror. In a second, she was in a wonderful world of fantasy, as her girlish body turned into a swan. Then came Prince Siegfried, who wore Benny Kessler's face, as she changed to Odette, Queen of the Maidens. They danced together tenderly, till dawn stole over the lake. Once more a swan, she glided away as the first side of the record ended. Her evening at her first ballet filled her imagination more vividly than ever and reflected itself in the mirror on the wall.

Bronna called from the third floor. "Rachel, come on up and see the bedrooms!"

The spell was broken. Waving her arms gracefully but regretfully to her reflection, Rachel ran upstairs.

As always, Bronna and she shared a bedroom. To Rachel's delight, the wallpaper, though faded, had a profusion of beautiful pink roses, her favorite flower.

Before Bronna had a chance to choose, Rachel said, "I'm sleeping on this side of the bed."

"You had the window side before," Bronna objected.

"I picked it first," Rachel argued.

"You didn't give me a chance."

"I'm older. I get first choice."

"Only two years older," Bronna cried.

They heard Hyman calling, "Look at my bedroom."

Bronna's sunny nature prevailed, a smile drying her tears as she ran into his room.

Rachel, glad to be alone, sat in her rocking chair. There was just enough space between the bed and the window for it to fit. She creaked away, comforted by this last familiar vestige in her bedroom of all the old furniture they had left behind. A soothing feeling enveloped her as she rocked, almost as though she were creeping out of her skin, and dancing.

She thought of all the changes, so many changes—even school. She and her brother and sister would continue Hebrew classes at the Talmud Torah on Catherine Street, but public school regulations required they attend school in their new district. Tomorrow was the first day at the new school, and at the mere thought butterflies flittered and skittered inside.

Hyman kept calling, and she was glad to be distracted.

"Look at the nice desk he's got," Bronna pointed as Rachel entered the room.

Grandly seated in front of his desk, he permitted Bronna, standing at his side, to push its roll-top lid up and down. Though markedly nicked and scarred, it looked more impressive than any desk she had ever seen. Hyman smiled happily. "See, I've got plenty of space to do my homework and sketching."

Rachel felt a wave of jealousy. He always got everything. If her parents had extra money, they'd probably spend it on him to study art. She would never get dance lessons. Before she had a chance to suppress her anger, the words came tumbling out.

"Bronna and I have to share a bedroom, yet you get the bigger one all to yourself. And now this great desk!"

"Yeah," echoed Bronna. "How come? It's not fair!"

Mama came out of her bedroom, which was next to Hyman's. She had overheard them. Rachel was glad.

Mama, however, said in an incredulous tone, as though surprised Rachel and Bronna questioned it—as though it were the most natural thing in the world for them to understand, "But he's the boy."

Rachel knew it was no use to protest further. Anyhow, did she really care about a desk and a bigger room?

How could she complain when her parents had singled her out for the most memorable birthday gift of all? Knowing how much dancing meant to her, even though they couldn't afford it, Mama scrimped for the tickets and Papa took her alone to the ballet. That proved how much her parents really loved her. They gave her an evening to treasure all her life. She was ashamed of herself. She would try not to forget again.

That night when they went to bed, Bronna, as usual, dropped off to sleep immediately. Rachel's thoughts flitted from the excitement of moving, to the new school tomorrow. So many different things were happening all at once. She looked around her surroundings, here in a small room, in a small house, on a small street. Would the sky above be too small for stars?

She opened her eyes wider to see the sky. And there they were—a thousand stars beckoning her as if saying:

> Beyond this street are stars
> Shining, glittering stars.

They would light her way tomorrow.

CHAPTER NINE

Rachel's heart pounded as she walked into the classroom the next morning. She waited for the teacher to acknowledge her, to take the introductory note from the office. But the teacher went on talking, while Rachel stood by her desk in front of the room. She felt every student's gaze appraising her critically. She didn't know what to do with her arms and legs, they were so heavy. She longed to sit down.

Finally, the teacher said, "Yes?"

Rachel handed her the note.

"Oh, you're the new pupil. Welcome." She smiled slightly. "I'm Miss Mallory. Class, this is Rachel Sussman. She has been transferred to us."

The ogling eyes of the children became bigger and bigger.

"Take your seat." Miss Mallory said, pointing to an empty one in the back of the room. "We're doing fractions, Rachel. I hope you can keep up. I'll check later on what you know."

Rachel stood rooted to the spot, paralyzed with fear. *Fractions?!* Arithmetic was her worst subject. They had started studying fractions in her old school and she couldn't get them through her head.

"Go! Take your seat," said Miss Mallory. "We have to get started."

A titter changed into a loud laughter as Rachel looked helplessly at Miss Mallory. From some unknown source of strength her legs moved, and she found her assigned seat and gladly sat down. The morning dragged by slowly as Miss Mallory explained the examples on the blackboard. Rachel did not understand a word of it.

Thank goodness I'm not sitting up front, she thought.

A girl in the first seat of the first row kept raising her hand when the teacher asked questions. When called upon, she gave the correct answers. Suddenly a bell rang out loudly. Miss Mallory nodded to the girl. "Ana, will you please erase the board?"

Ana rose from her seat and with mincing footsteps went to the blackboard. She's smart; she must be the teacher's pet, Rachel thought, admiring Ana's long, brown, curly hair, her stiffly starched pink dress. Rachel looked at her own dress, also pink, her favorite of the two she owned. She'd been pleased with it when she dressed earlier for this important day. But now, next to Ana's dress, it looked faded and worn.

By this time she couldn't concentrate on what Miss Mallory was saying, but kept her eyes pinned on the way the white collar and cuffs moved on her black wool dress.

Above the clanging of a second bell, she did hear Miss Mallory's words, "Class will go to recess. You may leave the room one row at a time."

As Rachel's row filed out, Miss Mallory said, "Rachel, please wait at my desk a moment."

Uh-oh, she's going to ask me about fractions, Rachel thought, terrified.

Miss Mallory turned to smile at Ana, who'd finished erasing the blackboard. "Since Rachel is new, would you please show her the girls' room and the yard where we have recess?"

Rachel breathed a grateful sigh of relief.

Miss Mallory flashed another smile at Ana. How pretty she is when she smiles, Rachel thought. The teacher's eyes, which seemed so icy but a moment ago, were now transformed to a soft, sky blue.

Rachel had dreaded recess, picturing herself standing alone in the yard, the object of curious stares. Instead, Ana took Rachel around and stayed with her the entire time.

"I saw you the day you moved in. We live on the same block," Ana said.

"We do?"

"We can go home from school together, and I'll show you where I live."

"Okay," Rachel said, gratefully.

"You have a brother and sister, don't you?"

"Yes."

"You're lucky. I'm an only child."

Rachel was surprised that Ana would find her lucky. As an only child, Rachel imagined, she could have anything she wanted.

"How do you like the class so far?" asked Ana.

Rachel liked to hear Ana's high melodic voice. She spoke slowly and weighed each word carefully before using it. I'll bet she takes elocution lessons, thought Rachel. She sounded just like her old schoolmate, Betsy Piper, who had taken them for years.

"I'm a little scared about the arithmetic," she admitted. "I'm not good with fractions."

"Oh, they're easy. I'll help you."

"Gosh," said Rachel, surprised. She expected Ana to be stuck-up like Betsy Piper, both so smart, so well-dressed. But here she was, as nice as could be. Friendly, even offering to help her with those horrible fractions. Standing beside her new friend as the March breezes licked about them, Rachel caught a faint whiff of lavender. It seemed to be coming from Ana's dress. She even smelled good.

"You're going to love Miss Mallory," said Ana.

"She seems kind of strict."

"Oh, no. It's such a large class and she's got so much work. But she's good, and fair. When I grow up I want to be a teacher, just like her."

Of course she likes Miss Mallory. Why shouldn't she? She's the teacher's favorite, Rachel thought. She remembered how Miss Mallory called upon Ana repeatedly, smiling so sweetly upon her.

"I'm going to be a dancer," she said. In her mind she whispered, I hope, oh, I hope.

As Ana and Rachel walked home for lunch, Ana stopped at the building Rachel had hoped, for a fleeting moment, was the teahouse the first day she'd come to the street. The sign painted on the storefront window read, "Abram's Dairy Restaurant;" shining-white Venetian blinds covered the window inside.

"Here's where I live. Let's walk back to school again," Ana called out to Rachel as she ran inside.

After eating hurriedly, Rachel went to Ana's. It was even nicer inside than outside. Ana's parents served dairy, and Rachel's parents served meat. To be strictly kosher, a restaurant had to be one or the other—you were not allowed to mix dairy and meat dishes. Rachel was glad there was no conflict. In her father's teahouse, most customers spoke Yiddish and wore working clothes. In Abram's Dairy Restaurant, white tablecloths covered the tables, the linoleum floor gleamed, even the customers looked different. The men wore neckties and jackets, and spoke English.

Ana's mother was in the kitchen.

"This is Rachel Sussman." Ana introduced her, smiling proudly.

"We're glad Ana has a friend her age nearby," her mother said. But she didn't look as though she meant it. She didn't smile a bit, merely looked at Rachel up and down so closely that she felt nervous beads of perspiration form above her upper lip. Hearing Ana's mother speak English, in the same slow, high-pitched voice as Ana's, surprised her. All her other friends' parents spoke mostly Yiddish, or English with an accent, as did Mama and Papa. Rachel couldn't wait to leave.

The afternoon school session passed quickly. First they had spelling. One of Rachel's favorite subjects, she excelled in it. But although she knew the words the teacher called out, she was too shy to raise her hand to answer. Then Miss Mallory went on to history, in which she explained about the signing of the Armistice in 1918, ending the Great War.

"It was the War to End All Wars," said the teacher.

How lucky she was to be living now, Rachel thought. After all the wars since time began, not to have to worry about another was reassuring.

Later, Miss Mallory beckoned to Rachel to sit beside her desk.

"Here's your copy of the book the class is reading," the teacher said, showing Rachel a slim novel of about a hundred and twenty-five pages. "We're almost finished."

Rachel reached for it.

"The assignment is to write a book report this weekend," Miss Mallory said. "I don't expect you to finish it, because you're starting late. But take it home and read as much as you can. See what you can do with it." With a glimmer of a smile, Rachel was dismissed.

Returning to her seat, she looked at the book. On the cover was a picture of a young ballerina about her age in a white tutu, "on point," slender arms gracefully curved over a head held high. Its title—*Dancing Dream.*

CHAPTER TEN

Creaking back and forth on her rocker, begrudging even time spent in eating, Rachel spent the entire weekend reading. She couldn't put the book down. It was about Elsie, an eleven year old orphan who wanted to be a dancer, and how her dancing dream came true.

Finally, finishing the last word on the last page, Rachel shut her eyes. Rocking slowly, she clutched the book against her heart. She was in a trance, fantasizing about her own dancing dream. She saw herself, a ballerina on stage before a spellbound audience.

Bronna burst into the bedroom clamoring, "Let's play jacks."

Startled, Rachel jumped, dropping the book. "Go away. I don't feel like it right now."

"Aw, c'mon," Bronna persisted, holding a handful of jacks in one hand, bouncing a little brown ball up and down in the other. "Aren't you tired of reading that stupid book Saturday and Sunday?"

In exasperation, Rachel replied, "Can't I have some privacy? I'm not in the mood."

Hyman stuck his head in their bedroom door, taunting, "What's the matter? Greta Garbo *vahnts* to be alone?"

"No chance of that around here," Rachel cried, retrieving her book. "Bronna, I can't play with you. I have to write a report."

"Please," wheedled Bronna, following closely as Rachel ran downstairs to the dining room. She spread out her book and tablet on the dining room table. Bronna sat next to her quietly, waiting for Rachel to finish.

As Rachel started writing, an avalanche of words poured out. She filled page after page, ending with—"I'm glad Elsie's dancing dream came true. It gives me hope. For this is also my dream."

As she read and reread what she had written, Hyman came into the room whistling loudly. Then she heard the plop, plop of Bronna's ball on the table.

"Hush," she said. "Don't you see I'm trying to do my homework?"

Bronna hesitated a moment but the plop, plop of the ball started again. Hyman whistled louder than ever.

"Stop it," Rachel screeched.

"I'm doing my homework, too," Hyman said, blue eyes widening innocently. He continued whistling, placing his arithmetic book and a sheet of paper opposite her at the dining room table.

"Why is everybody annoying me?" Rachel demanded. "Your desk is upstairs, Hyman."

"So what? I'd rather work here. You can't stop me."

"I can't concentrate with you whistling."

Would you rather hear me sing?" Hyman grinned, then chanted, "Rachel, Rachel, new in class, she's so dumb, she won't pass!"

"I'm going to tell Mama and Papa that both of you are bothering me," Rachel cried furiously. But they knew she wouldn't, because their parents were so busy in the store.

"How about the harmonica?" Hyman grinned, taking it out of his shirt pocket, playing it as loudly as possible.

Rachel aimed her book, ready to throw it at him, shouting, "Stop it, you buck-tooth, four-eyed, pesky..."

Bronna grabbed the book. "He's only teasing. He doesn't mean it, Rachel," she said contritely.

Although Rachel was ashamed of her tears, she couldn't stop them. Softhearted Bronna patted her. "Please don't cry—we love you."

Rachel sobbed louder and louder.

"I'm sorry," Hyman blurted. "You know I'm always kidding. Guess I really don't want to be upstairs alone even with my very own desk." He paused. Rachel stopped crying.

"It's so quiet," Hyman continued. "I miss doing our homework in the old kitchen, with Mama and Papa and everybody around the table. Everything's so different now."

Bronna looked suspiciously on the verge of tears.

"It's all right," said Rachel, getting up to hug her sister and brother. "I guess I'm on edge with all these changes, too. But I try so hard, and I'm worried about the new school. Can't you understand?"

Chastened, Hyman returned to his arithmetic, Bronna beside him. Rachel tried to reread her book report but her brother's words, "Everything's different now," kept ringing in her ears.

He's right, she thought. It felt so strange for the three of them to be doing homework in the dining room, with Mama and Papa always downstairs now, working in the store. She missed the old times—being with their parents in the kitchen after supper. Not that they could help with homework, but they were there. She heard Papa's continual refrain, "You children are lucky to be in America and have a chance to get an education. Take advantage of it." And, Mama, invariably repeating the same words for emphasis.

Now their whole way of life was changed. Mama and Papa were in the store seven days a week, sometimes too busy to sit with them when they ate at their table in the back of the store. Rachel, Bronna, and Hyman had to fend for themselves and try not to give Mama and Papa any trouble.

They heard Mama's footsteps.

"I'm glad to see you're doing your homework together," she smiled approvingly, huffing from the climb. "I just came up to get a clean apron. I spilled gravy on this one and it's a mess."

"I'll get the apron for you, Mama," offered Bronna.

"No, that's all right, Bronna. You don't know where I keep them."

"I know where they are," said Rachel, already on the stairs to the third floor. Since Mama's face looked awfully red, flushed from the heat and cooking in the hot kitchen, Rachel wanted to save her the steps.

"We may be poor, but we're clean," Mama said as Rachel held the fresh apron open for her. "I do want to say, Rachel, that Papa and I are pleased with the way you're helping. Taking care of your own clothes, making the beds, dusting. We're glad we can depend on you." She didn't say, After all, Hyman's a boy and Bronna's too young, but Rachel knew what she meant.

"That's all right," she said. It was hard to be the middle child, stuck with all the chores, but maybe helping out would mean extra money for dancing lessons.

Mama finished tying the bow on her apron. She asked Hyman, who was bending over his books, "How are you coming along with your Bar Mitzvah studies?"

"Okay, Mama." Blue eyes blinking behind his glasses, he smiled, "I told the Rabbi my Uncle Yossel was a cantor in New York and he said he was looking forward to meeting him. Is he coming?"

"He hasn't written. But he'd better." Patting his back, Mama added, "Go ahead, study. The Bar Mitzvah will be here before you know it. Don't worry about coming down to help Papa tonight. If we get busy, I'll call Rachel."

Rachel protested, "That's his job."

"The store is everyone's job," Mama snapped.

"How about Bronna?" Without waiting for an answer, Rachel added, "I know, I know. She's too young."

"That's right," Mama affirmed.

Rachel felt everything being piled on her shoulders. She hated helping in the store—the gaping faces, everybody talking loudly, all taking her away from dancing practice.

Mama sighed, speaking softly as though to herself. "It's a shame to have to give up living private, work so hard, yet still worry about meeting expenses. Still, Papa's happier; he has his own business and is independent."

Rachel felt worse than ever. Her hopes for dancing lessons, which had flared when Mama spoke about being pleased with her a moment ago, crumbled. How could she ask her parents for extra money? Yet she was getting older. It would soon be too late for her to even start. Her muscles would be too tight. She was farther away from her dancing dream than ever. Even Elsie, the girl in the story, was luckier than she. Guilt swept over her. How could she compare herself with Elsie, who was an orphan? She wouldn't trade her family for anything. But it would almost take a miracle to get those lessons.

She went into the quiet of the parlor. Even in the dark, she saw the phonograph. She put on her record. Her feet automatically responded to the music. She danced slowly, then faster, then slowly again. Leaping, bending, pirouetting, all else was forgotten as she retreated into a world of glorious sound and motion.

"Rachel, we need you downstairs." Mama's voice returned her to reality. Most reluctantly, she stopped dancing, turned off the record player, and gently shut the parlor door. Her precious domain would have to wait until she returned.

She passed Hyman and Bronna, heads bent over their books at the dining room table. They looked so cozy. Wish I could stay upstairs, too, she thought, but Papa needs me.

It was very busy in the teahouse, the customers clamoring for attention. Papa, after frantically taking supper orders, dashed to the kitchen to help Mama fill them, as the cook had already left. "You can set up and clear the tables," he said.

Her father never called upon the children. If Rachel happened to be in the store at a busy time and pitched in of her own volition, his eyes flashed with gratitude.

But Mama, acting as a sentry in the kitchen, summoned them whenever necessary. "So I'll be the bad one," she said to Papa. "If it were up to you, you'd do all the work yourself. God forbid you disturb your children or take them away from their studies."

Rachel remembered how gray Sam looked the first day they had visited the teahouse. How she never wanted Papa to get like that. Yet, after only a few weeks in business, Papa looked so tired. And what was she doing? Dancing! Guilt made her feet fly as she rushed to help. So much to do—put slices of Mama's homemade bread on each table, silverware, napkins, take the orders.

"An order of meat, potatoes, *kasha*, and gravy," she called to Mama above the din, as Papa came out of the kitchen with a brimming bowlful of hot soup.

"Is that a way to serve soup?" Mama shouted at Papa's retreating back. "How do you expect to make a profit?" To Rachel, she added, sighing, "The bowl is overflowing, like his heart."

A moment later, while heaping dirty dishes on the kitchen table for Frank, the dishwasher, Rachel again heard Mama complaining as Papa lavishly filled a platter.

"Mister, take it easy. Let me make up the orders."

"This is for Alex," Papa said.

"Oh, so how long is he going to eat for nothing?"

"You know he's looking for a job, Dora."

"Can I help it if he's not working? What is it here, the Salvation Army?"

"*Shaah*," Papa pleaded. "He'll hear you. He's a fine man. He'll pay us back when he finds work."

"All right, all right, so Alex is a fine man. What's the matter you're feeding Dempsey, that no-goodnik who left his wife?"

"Ahh, you're wrong, Dora. Poor Dempsey's a sick man. He didn't leave his wife. She left him. It's a *mitzvah*, a blessing, to help him. When he gets back on his feet, that will be payment enough for us."

"Speak for yourself," Mama moaned, shaking her head. "No wonder the customers love you. Those loafers. No wonder we can't pay our bills. What will become of us?"

"Thank God we have our own business during this Depression and can help a few unfortunates who have nowhere else to go but the river. We'll manage. Don't worry."

Rachel noticed how, as each customer entered the door, their eyes searched out Papa. No matter how busy, he acknowledged every one with a smile or gesture, like he greeted his children when coming home. She worked even harder to help him, save him as many steps as possible. Soon, everyone was served and things weren't so hectic. She began clearing off the dirty dishes and wiping the tabletops until they gleamed.

She trudged into the kitchen with a tray overloaded with dirty dishes. A cup fell to the floor. Picking it up, she sighed with relief that it wasn't broken. Her mother shook her hands at her, and shouted, "Be careful! You're such a *klutz*."

Rachel was crushed. Imagine calling a ballerina clumsy! It was the worst insult. Hurt tears overflowed. Papa, coming into the kitchen at that moment, overheard.

"For God's sake, Dora," he said. "Leave her alone! She's so good, tries so hard to please, and you're always at her." He stomped out of the kitchen.

Papa so rarely lost his temper that Rachel was afraid Mama would be angrier than ever at her. Amazingly, her mother came to her, and put her arms around her. "Papa's right," she said. "I don't know what devil drives me." Her voice faltered. "I expect so much from you and depend on you the same way my mother did with me. She was sometimes harsh, and would get excited, too. It was just her way—and I guess it's also mine. She didn't mean it, but never had a chance to tell me so, dying as suddenly as she did."

She pressed Rachel harder to her. "But I want you to know, Rachel, I don't know what I'd do without you."

Rachel was thrilled by Mama's words, feeling as if a tremendous weight had been lifted. Realizing that there was nothing she wouldn't do for her parents, she returned to the tables, cleaning them more diligently than ever.

The customers were relaxing, drinking their *glezela tai*, listening to the news commentator on the radio. As she worked, she heard chilling words drift around the warm room. "...Adolf Hitler, Chancellor of Germany...Nazi party...anti-Semitism...Jews...refugees..."

The teacher had told them in class that the situation in Germany was worsening. Mama was worried about her family in Hungary—it was a problem that could spread.

Dreyfus, from the kitchen card games, was having dinner. He was devouring a thick, perfectly-broiled-to-a-pink ribsteak, smothered with fried onions, drenched with garlic and pepper. Mama's specialty. He smiled as Rachel passed his table. "How's our beautiful dancer?" he asked.

She looked around to see if perhaps he was addressing someone else. Except for Papa, no one called her beautiful, with her brown eyes, short, straight brown hair, and skinny body. Beautiful was Bronna—blonde, curly hair framing sea-blue eyes, her up-tilted nose. She immediately forgave him for not letting her perform at the last kitchen card game.

Maxie stood behind an empty chair motioning to Dreyfus, shouting, "I'm saving this place for you." His cronies, Dave and Reds, were already seated, waiting for him. Dreyfus's ruddy face reddened more than ever in his haste to finish and get to the domino table.

The fourth man at the table was Farmer, so named because he owned a farm in Vineland, New Jersey. How he did any work on the farm was a mystery, since he spent most of his time in the teahouse, usually at the domino table. The rumor was that his wife ran the farm and was glad to be rid of him. He stood out from the other customers, impeccably dressed in a pin-striped suit and sporting a well-kept mustache waxed at the ends.

The domino game started. Standing next to Maxie and watching the game was Handfinger, one of their best customers. He slept in a rooming-house down the street. The rest of his time he spent in the store, eating all of his meals there and playing or watching the domino games. He was old and fat, his yellow-toothed smile enigmatic. Newly retired from the rag business, he loved to flash his wallet, thick with twenty and fifty dollar bills, casually bragging, "I didn't get a chance to go the bank today."

Mama always said he was a miser. "He screams the loudest when he loses a quarter in the game. He has to be handled with kid gloves."

As Rachel observed them at the domino table, Papa patted the top of her head. "Thanks for your help, Racheleh. You can go now."

She was halfway up the stairs, when Dreyfus started shouting, "Farmer! You dirty, rotten son of a ..."

Mama ran out of the kitchen, waving her spoon above her head. "Hey, no cursing allowed! There are young girls here. This is a respectable place."

"Let me at him, the *momser!*" shouted Dreyfus.

Rachel ran back down the stairs, her heart thumping wildly. Papa was flinging his one hundred and fifty pounds against the two hundred and fifty pound Dreyfus. The commotion even brought Hyman and Bronna down. Bronna rushed bravely straight to Papa's side, her little fists flailing away at Dreyfus.

"What happened?" a white-faced Hyman asked Rachel.

Rachel, unable to answer, grabbed Hyman's hand.

Dreyfus yelled, "I work too hard on the pushcarts to lose my money this way. Let me at him."

Skinny Dave stood protectively in front of Farmer, who crouched behind him, feverishly twirling the waxed ends of his mustache.

Rachel was sickened to see customers enjoying the confrontation. Handfinger's eyes glistened with excitement. Worst of all, no one came to help Papa except Bronna. Even she and Hyman were too scared to move. And so, apparently, was Mama, in spite of her being furious about them making bets.

"Behave yourself or I'll throw you out," Papa threatened, shaking his fist at them.

Rachel thought that was a crazy remark. Papa could barely restrain Dreyfus, who seemed to swell up larger than ever as he glared at Farmer.

"Farmer," Papa shouted. "No cheating here. You understand?"

Rachel was surprised to see Dreyfus sit down, obviously pleased that Papa took his part. He picked up his dominoes and resumed playing.

Everyone watched Farmer suspiciously as he slouched into his seat.

Smiling reassuringly at Rachel and her brother and sister, Papa went back to work. Mama ducked into the kitchen. The other customers continued their political discussion of the moment.

Rachel heaved a heavy sigh of relief as she followed Hyman and Bronna upstairs. Imagine, she'd been so angry with them earlier, yet now her heart felt full of love. She was so proud of Bronna for protecting Papa, and grateful that Hyman was there beside her, holding her hand.

Back to the privacy of upstairs. To the parlor, to her record. She could dance with a clear conscience; she had earned the right.

CHAPTER ELEVEN

Rachel opened her eyes Monday morning to the sun shining through her bedroom window, bright with the promise of a lovely spring day.

She'd worn the pink dress on Friday, so it was the blue one's turn today. It was draped over her rocking chair. Since Mama was so busy in the store, taking care of her clothes was Rachel's own responsibility now.

She stopped in the kitchen to say good morning to Mama, before joining Hyman and Bronna, already eating breakfast in the teahouse. Mama's keen eyes, always inspecting, looked over the blue dress. Finally, she said, "You look nice, Rachel. We may be poor, but we're clean."

Rachel was pleased.

Papa was in and out of the kitchen taking customer's orders, setting up for the day's business, but not too busy to stop and smile at her, his eyes beaming with pride.

Mama brought a bowl of hot oatmeal to Rachel, urging, "Eat. Eat. You're too thin and still growing. You need strength for that dancing you're always doing."

"Ballerinas are thin," called out Becky, a regular patron sitting nearby. By now, Rachel was used to the customers taking a special interest in everything she and her brother and sister did. "You wouldn't think it to look at me now," Becky continued, "but when I was young, I wanted to be a dancer, too."

Rachel found it hard to believe that this emaciated, bedraggled lady with orange-red hair had once been a young girl with the same desire as hers.

Becky's friend, Clara, sitting beside her, giggled. She was her complete opposite—fat, with hair black as shoe polish. Clara's son, Jake, looked exactly like his mother—a younger, male version. Although in his early thirties, he huddled as close to his mother as a young child. The three were inseparable. They slept in a rooming-house nearby, spending every waking hour in the store, always at the same corner table.

Clara's giggle turned to hilarious laughter.

"Look who wanted to be a dancer," she said, her pudgy hand pointing to Becky.

Jake, following his mother's lead, banged on the table with all his brute strength. His face swelled dark purple as he laughed loudly.

Rachel, busy watching them, forgot she hated oatmeal and gulped it down.

"Look who's laughing," shrieked Becky. "Two *meshuginas!*"

"Don't you call my son crazy," Clara yelled, standing over him protectively.

"Is retarded better?"

"They'll break the table," Mama protested as Papa ran to them.

"*Shaah*," he cautioned them. "Don't make a scene. Others are eating their breakfast."

"I told you before to throw them out, Berel," Mama said. "Between those three and the domino commotion, how can you expect decent customers to come here?"

Although Rachel laughed along with everyone else, she knew Mama was right. You'd never see customers like them in Ana's parents' restaurant.

"Their money is as good as anybody's. It's not a fancy place for fancy people here."

Mama grumbled, "Who else but you would put up with them?" But Rachel was glad to see the dimple finding its way back into Mama's cheeks as she returned to the kitchen.

Hyman muttered, "What a bunch of characters." Pushing his empty bowl aside, he pulled a small pad from his back pocket and started sketching.

Bronna edged closer to watch him. Rachel was fascinated at the thought of a younger Becky, daring to dream of being a ballerina.

In a few seconds the sketch was finished. Hyman held it up for Bronna and Rachel to see. It was unmistakably Becky, Clara, and Jake.

"Oh, my goodness. It's exactly like them," Rachel gasped.

Bronna called to Papa, "Look what Hyman did."

Busy Papa stopped. Bronna, reaching to his waist, seized the opportunity, now rare, to put her arms around her father's long legs and hold him captive as she snuggled affectionately against him. Rachel got a good warm feeling to see Papa's eyes shine, his lips stretch into a seemingly endless smile as he studied the sketch.

Papa marched into the kitchen carrying the sketch—Rachel, Hyman, and Bronna trailing behind—to show it to Mama.

"An artist, a genius we've got," Mama crowed. Stepping away from the hot stove, she put down the platter she was preparing and gave Hyman an enthusiastic hug and kiss.

Mrs. Cohen, the cook, also gave her opinion. "He certainly is talented."

Frank, the dishwasher, who could speak no English, barked something in Polish. Rachel interpreted it as signifying elaborate approval.

"And to think," Mama laughed, "when he was only five I used to scold him for scribbling on the floor. Till one day, Mrs. Bomerantz said, 'What are you doing? He's trying to draw a horse and wagon.' The very next day Papa brought home a blackboard and he's been drawing ever since."

Back into the tearoom Papa went with the sketch, the children at his heels. He had to show off to the customers. First the domino table where, as usual, Maxie, Dave, Dreyfus and Reds sat, playing a fast after-breakfast game before going to work. They stopped politely to look at the sketch.

Rachel stared in fascination at the half-chewed cigar in Dreyfus's thick lips. It never budged an inch as he said, "Hyman's really got a good likeness."

Maxie stretched his short arm to pat Hyman's shoulder. Dave smiled broadly, the Adam's apple bulging. Reds gave Hyman a bright, shiny quarter, saying, "Good boy." Rachel watched Reds hesitate, looking at Bronna and her. In a moment his hand was in his pocket again. "And here's something for Bronna, our reluctant singer, and Rachel, the dancer." He pressed a nickel into each girl's palm. Papa nodded. It was okay for them to accept.

Papa carefully tacked the sketch on the wall behind the register, beside several of Hyman's other sketches. Some customers edged up closely to examine it.

Since selling the teahouse, Sam now came in as a regular early in the morning. He looked at the picture, too. "It's good," he said, and went into a paroxysm of wheezing and coughing, his gray mustache fluttering feebly.

"Not bad," Handfinger admitted.

"Hyman's got talent," the customers unanimously raved.

"That's us in the picture," Jake sheepishly acknowledged. Becky and Clara stood up and took mock bows to the spontaneous applause of the customers.

"I've got to get back to work," said Papa. "Time for school, children."

On the way, Rachel stopped to pick up Ana.

"Did you read the book, *Dancing Dream*, that we had for homework?" Ana asked in her high, sweet voice.

"Yes, I did."

"You read the whole thing in one weekend?"

"I did the book report on it, too."

"Really?"

83

"Uh-huh."

"Rachel, that's wonderful."

Out of the corner of her eye Rachel noticed that the yellow ribbon in Ana's hair was the identical color as her dress. She always looked so bright and fresh. Next to her, Rachel's dress looked pale and washed-out. Mama's words, 'We may be poor, but we're clean,' echoed in her ear, but they didn't make her feel better. She was happy to have Ana as a friend, but somewhat in awe of her. She couldn't help wonder why Ana, who was so smart and wore such lovely clothes, wanted her for a friend.

"You know something?" Ana said. "I think the greatest thing in the world is to have a sister and brother. It's awful being an only child."

"Doesn't an only child get everything she wants?"

"Who cares? It's lonely. When I get married, I'm going to have ten children."

Rachel's heart swelled. For the first time she felt sorry for Ana. Though they got on her nerves sometimes, she couldn't picture life without Bronna, who was so adorable, and Hyman, so smart, such a talented artist. She did love them so.

"Do you have a boyfriend?" asked Ana.

"I like somebody but he doesn't know it," confided Rachel. The mere thought of Benny Kessler made her warm all over.

"Me, too," cried Ana.

Rachel like Ana better than ever. The smell of sweet springtime was everywhere. It felt good to be alive. She played the game of making sure not to step on the bits of grass struggling to grow between the cement cracks on the pavement. It was all she could do to refrain from taking Ana's hand and dancing to school.

Miss Mallory was at her desk, looking strict as ever as the children filed in. "Good morning, class," she said.

"Good morning, Miss Mallory," Rachel and the class replied in loud, fresh, Monday-morning voices.

The teacher collected their homework. She started the first lesson—fractions. Rachel was delighted to find she was more comfortable in class. Later in the afternoon she even answered a spelling question.

When the final bell rang, Miss Mallory called, "Rachel Sussman, please stay after class."

Immediately, Rachel became nervous. She couldn't imagine what the teacher wanted.

Miss Mallory pointed to a chair beside her desk. "Sit down, Rachel."

Rachel sat, her gaze averted, afraid to look into Miss Mallory's face and perhaps see an even grimmer look than before.

"Since you're new in class, I wanted to get an idea of your work. I looked at your book report during lunch. Here, I've marked it," she said, handing it back to Rachel.

Rachel reached for the report. A large "A" in red ink was on the top of the page. Her cheeks burned. She turned to the last page where she had ended her report with the words, "I am glad Elsie's dancing dream came true. It gives me hope. For this is my dream, also."

Miss Mallory had written in red, "I, too, hope your dream comes true."

Rachel looked into the teacher's face. Blue eyes, diamond-bright and sparkling, were smiling at her. She dabbed at her tears, unprepared for the excellent mark, the smile, the kindness.

Miss Mallory asked, "If you have such a strong desire, what have you done to make it come true? Have you taken dancing lessons?"

Rachel whispered, "N-no."

"Why not?"

"My parents can't afford it. I wouldn't even dare to ask."

Miss Mallory's face brightened. Her words came slowly. "Did you ever hear of the Arts Center?"

"No."

"It's that red brick building with the iron gate at Third and Arch Streets. Five blocks away."

"We just moved. I don't know the neighborhood."

"Well, they do have dance classes. And I believe a few scholarships are awarded, based on talent. Why don't you try out?"

Rachel's eyes and mouth opened wide. "You mean I might be able to get a scholarship? Not have to pay?"

The teacher smiled radiantly, saying in a most positive tone, "Rachel Sussman, life doesn't promise you anything." Her white fingers, whose long, pink nails matched her pink button earrings and dress, raised Rachel's chin so she could look straight into her student's eyes. She continued, "But don't you ever stop reaching for the highest ring on the merry-go-round!"

The fragrance of lilacs from Miss Mallory enveloped Rachel. Her heart raced. She exclaimed, "I want to dance. I want lessons more than anything."

"If your talent is half as great as your desire, you are going to take lessons. At the Arts Center. And if not there, somewhere," Miss Mallory said firmly.

Luckily, there was no Hebrew school this afternoon because of a teacher's meeting. She was free to go directly to the Arts Center.

Rachel was surprised to see Ana waiting for her in the schoolyard.

"What happened? What did Miss Mallory want?" she asked.

"Oh, Ana." Rachel breathlessly repeated what Miss Mallory had told her. "I'm walking right over to see what I can find out. I can't wait." She was trembling all over.

"I'll go with you," said Ana, putting her arm in Rachel's to keep up with her quick stride. "It's not too far. I heard about the Arts Center. This rich, old man died and left his home as a school for the arts."

Rachel barely listened. When they reached the Arts Center, Ana waited as she went to the woman behind a desk in the lobby.

"I, uh, I want to find out about the dance classes," she blurted.

The woman squinted at a chart on her desk blotter. "They're held on Friday."

"Um, I'd like to apply for a scholarship. I mean, what do I do?"

"Have you been here before?"

"No. My teacher sent me here."

"Well, you just can't come marching in and go right to class. I'll have to ask you a few questions first."

Rachel swallowed.

"Name? Address? Grade in school? Father's occupation?" Before she answered one question came the next—sharp, fast.

Rachel, drenched with perspiration, anticipated a tough question any second.

"All right. Here's your card. It has to be signed by your mother or father where I've checked in red. The dance teacher will talk with you two weeks from Friday. You'll be given a chance to try out. Next."

Clutching the precious card tightly, Rachel walked around the lobby for a few moments with Ana, looking at information posted on the walls about various classes. Perhaps they had an art class for Hyman. Or something for Bronna. By the time she got home, the card was limp from having been incessantly taken in and out of her pocket for inspection.

"Guess what! I'm going to try out for a dance scholarship," Rachel shouted as she entered her father's establishment. Hyman, Bronna, Mama, and Papa gathered at their table in back of the store.

The customers crowded around them and listened. By this time, they were like family, and Rachel was accustomed to their interest and input. She gave them the details all in one breath.

"See, I told you America is a golden land of opportunity," Papa said, tousling Rachel's hair affectionately. "You're going to get that scholarship. You'll be a ballerina."

"I'm not sure I'll get it—don't get your hopes up," cautioned Rachel. But in her heart she prayed Papa was right.

"Nobody has better dancing schools than Russia," said Becky, of the orange-red hair, who wanted to be a ballerina in her youth. "They have the best teachers and the best dancers."

"What are you? A Communist?" sputtered Handfinger. "Nothing's wrong with Philadelphia's teachers and dancers."

Rachel was disappointed in Mama's reaction. She didn't seem excited, and was even hesitant. "I don't know," she said. "Dancing is not a life for a Jewish girl. I'm against it."

Rachel's heart dropped as Mama continued. "Where I come from in Hungary, it was unheard of to be a dancer."

"But this is America," said Handfinger. "Let her try for the scholarship, at least."

The customers surrounding the table agreed. "Yes, let her try."

Mama turned her head to frown at them. "We've lived in this city all these years and never heard of the Arts Center, scholarships. It don't sound kosher."

"All right, Dora, let's give Rachel her chance," said Papa, as he painstakingly signed his name on the card.

"We'd better get back to work, Berel. The cook leaves early, and it's almost suppertime," was Mama's way of dismissing the subject.

"Yep, I guess so," said Papa, lingering a moment longer to give Rachel an extra pat on the head. Slowly disentangling his long legs from beneath the table, he got up and busied himself again in the store.

"Well. Now, whaddaya think about that?" was Hyman's slow, thoughtful remark. Then with a big smile, he said, "I'm glad. I know how much it means to you."

"Can I try for a singing scholarship?" squealed Bronna.

"Sure." Rachel was so happy, she wanted everyone else to be, also. "And you could try for a scholarship, too, Hyman. They have all kinds of art classes at the Center."

He heaved a sigh. "I can't apply right now. I'm doing all this extra art work at home for the school paper. And even with my Bar Mitzvah over next week, Mama and Papa expect me to continue my religious studies. Maybe Yeshiva. After all, I'm the son—the oldest."

"They probably won't let me go to the Arts Center because they'll say I'm too young," said Bronna.

Whew, Rachel thought to herself, much relieved. Although Mama was disapproving, she wasn't forbidding. She did let Papa sign for her to try out for the scholarship. This was one of those rare times she felt lucky to be the middle child.

CHAPTER TWELVE

The week dragged by. Everyday after school Rachel hurriedly finished her homework, and the teahouse and household chores. Then she spent hours by the mirror practicing for the tryout.

Friday afternoon she was helping in the store when the door opened and in walked Uncle Yossel. Overjoyed, she ran to him. "Uncle! We didn't know for sure whether you were coming."

Papa greeted him with a warm handshake, eyes crinkling in an extra-special smile. Mama, rushing out of the kitchen, wiped her hands on her apron before crushing him to her with a kiss.

Rachel called Bronna and Hyman from upstairs. "Come down. Look who's here."

Everyone hugged and kissed as Mama cried, "But why didn't we hear from you? You didn't answer my letters."

Gruffly, speaking in Yiddish, with not one trace of a smile, as though almost two years hadn't elapsed since he saw them, he said, "You don't think I'd miss Hyman's Bar Mitzvah tomorrow, do you?"

"Have you heard from the family in Hungary?" asked Mama anxiously. "I haven't had an answer to my last letter."

"Things look bad for them and all the Jews with that Hitler and the Nazis," said Uncle Yossel. "I'm waiting for a letter, too."

"We'll just have to wait and see," said Mama.

Mama sighed. Uncle Yossel looked troubled.

Rachel remembered the teacher telling the class about Hitler and the Nazis. She worried about the family in Hungary, and hoped her mother would get a letter from them soon.

Mama was always telling them stories about the family she left behind in Hungary. She was the oldest, and of her three brothers, Hersh, Yossel, Hillel, and her sister Goldie, Yossel was the only one who came to America. He was forever soliciting money to send to the family there. "I don't make much but give more than I can afford, and you have to, also," was his cry. "They need it badly!" And Mama and Papa eked out to Yossel as much as they could.

Because he worked in New York City he visited them rarely, but when he did, it was truly a gala event. They were so happy to see him. And proud. It didn't matter to Rachel that he came empty-handed, but Papa, who never found fault with people, would say to Mama, "How does an uncle come without a little something, a *tsatstke*, a toy for the children?" In the same breath he continued, "So, all right, he loves the family in his own way. But it's a *shanda*, a disgrace. The man makes a living as a cantor, yet his clothes are threadbare and that old rumbleseat car he drives barely made the trip here in one piece."

Mama made the usual excuses. Yossel was gassed as a young soldier in the War in Europe, which she said accounted for his many odd ways. "So he's eccentric. So he's stingy. He's got a good heart, he loves us, and we love him. He's family."

"Come, Dora," said Papa, taking her by the hand. "Yossel hasn't seen our teahouse yet. Let's show him around."

All business stopped, even the game at the domino table, as Mama and Papa led him on a guided tour. The customers gaped.

"So this is the golden-voiced cantor from New York," whispered Maxie.

"Maybe he'll sing something for us," said Reds.

"Maybe 'Eli, Eli,'" said Dreyfus. "I love that one."

Food-conscious as ever, Mama set a platter in front of Uncle Yossel. "You must be starved. It's a long ride from New York."

Without further ado he attended to his plate while Rachel and her family, the customers, the cook, and the dishwasher grouped around him, watching.

"Hyman looks more like his bachelor uncle every day," said Mama.

It was true, Rachel marveled. Hyman was a young carbon copy of Uncle Yossel. The same blue eyes with glasses, same dark brown hair, and an identical large cleft carved in a square chin.

Between mouthfuls Uncle Yossel looked up to ask, "How's your drawing coming along?"

In response, Hyman pulled a small pad from his back pocket. Eyes in narrow slits, tip of his tongue by the side of his lips, he sketched Uncle Yossel with quick, firm pencil strokes. Everyone watched. In a few moments the drawing was complete and Hyman held it up. The likeness was almost like a photograph.

"That's a God-given talent you have, Hyman," Uncle Yossel pronounced. "I'm keeping this with the rest of the sketches you've made of me."

Rachel wanted to get another look and moved closer.

Uncle Yossel put the sketch in his pocket, saying, "Yep, Hyman's a Kretzenberger. He has our father's talent, Dora. Remember how he struggled making a living as a bricklayer? Once in a while getting the chance to paint pictures on rich people's walls."

"See," Mama said to the customers, the cook, and the dishwasher. "What did I tell you?"

Everyone looked impressed.

Bronna, impatient for attention, crept onto Uncle Yossel's lap. Laughing heartily, he held her close as she hugged him in her uninhibited way, planting wet kisses on his face.

Holding her at arm's length, he said, "Bronna's a little Kretzenberger, too. Got the blue eyes, and her mother's blonde hair."

Squinting his eyes he looked at Rachel. "Who do you take after? All the Kretzenbergers have blue eyes—yours are brown."

"She looks like my mother," said Papa.

"And I'm named after your mother, so I'm a composite," Rachel informed him, laughing. She felt so happy. It was so good to see Mama's brother, their one relative in America.

Dreyfus, apparently unable to contain himself, called out, "How about a song, Yossel? Sing 'Eli, Eli' for us?"

"Yes, yes!" The customers took up the clamor.

Uncle Yossel stared at them, blue eyes suddenly icy. "No! I never sing on a full stomach," he growled ungraciously. He blew at a glass of hot tea Mama set before him, and took a sip.

The cook and the dishwasher went back to the kitchen, the customers to the tables. Mama and Papa led Uncle Yossel upstairs. When he entered the parlor, he roared, "I can't believe it! Three children and no piano?"

"A piano they need? Lucky they have bread and butter in these hard times," Mama replied.

"Some things are more important than food," said Uncle Yossel. "I'm going out—I'll be back soon."

Rachel spent a peaceful hour alone in the parlor, dancing to her *Swan Lake* record. Hearing a commotion above the music, she looked out the window. To her great surprise, she saw Mama, Papa, Bronna, Hyman, the customers, and a growing crowd of curious onlookers outside their house.

They were watching Uncle Yossel wildly waving his hands and shouting directions to a few burly, iron-muscled men removing a piano from a truck. She hurried out to join them.

"Oh, my goodness. A piano! For us?" Rachel asked.

She watched as the men removed the window from the second floor to make space for the piano to go through. For protection, they covered it with an old quilt. They clambered onto the roof, and secured a pulley, threaded with a heavy rope, which they tied around the piano. The movers' faces were distorted with strain as slowly but surely they carefully hoisted it through the second floor window.

The piano was placed in a dark, empty corner of the parlor. The spot seemed to come alive, as though it had been just waiting for the stately, mahogany piano.

Their job done, the movers followed everyone down to the store where they presented the bill to Uncle Yossel.

He scrutinized it very carefully and then turned it over to Papa. "Pay the men," he ordered.

Papa's face paled. "But this is thirty-five dollars!"

Uncle Yossel nodded. "It's a bargain."

"I can't believe I'm hearing right," Mama screamed. "That's all we need now is a piano we have to pay for ourselves."

"What are you crying about? They practically gave it away. A secondhand player piano that looks new. Even threw in piano rolls for nothing."

"Yossel, we don't have money for a piano. We're lucky if we can pay our bills!"

"Always complaining. Children have to have a piano in the house. You found the money for the teahouse. Borrow the money, get it from somewhere."

Rachel was embarrassed. Everyone was listening as Mama's and Uncle Yossel's voices grew louder and louder. She was sure she heard laughter. She remembered that no sooner did Uncle Yossel arrive, then he and Mama always would quarrel about something.

Suddenly, Handfinger, in spite of his miserly reputation, pulled out his wallet. Painstakingly counting out thirty-five crisp bills, he handed them to Papa saying, "Yossel's right. Children need a piano in the house. Here's the money, Berel. You can pay me back a dollar a week."

"Good. I'll write you up an I.O.U. note right away," Uncle Yossel said importantly.

Papa raised his eyebrows in resigned acceptance. Nothing Yossel said or did surprised him. "Thanks, Handfinger," he said, shaking his customer's hand.

94

"I wouldn't do it for anyone else but you," Handfinger replied loudly. He looked pointedly at the other customers, who were exchanging incredulous stares.

Rachel overheard one of them saying, "I see it, but I don't believe it. Berel must be an angel for Handfinger to part with his money like that."

Another customer laughed, "That Yossel, he may be a cantor, and learned in Hebrew, but he's a real character!"

Mama muttered, "Yossel, you'll never change."

"Nag, nag, nag. How do you stand it, Berel?" Uncle Yossel asked. "Come children," he said motioning to them. "Let's go upstairs and play the piano."

Rachel couldn't believe they owned a piano. It was so beautiful. Her uncle sat down on the stool. "See, this is the way you play—I taught myself," he cried. Fingers crashing on the keys, he played "My Yiddishe Mama," his cantorial voice soaring above the music.

"Let me hear the songs you've learned in Hebrew school," he said to the children. They sang "Shalom Aleichem," "Hatikvah," and "Bim Bam" as he accompanied them on the piano, singing along with them. He then played some popular tunes, including "Happy Days Are Here Again," which they all sang with great gusto.

Rachel was delighted with the three rolls of music that came with the piano, even though some of them were very old pieces. "Sweet Georgia Brown," "Am I Blue?" and "Three O'clock in The Morning." She and her brother and sister took turns playing them over and over until it was time for Friday night services.

Uncle Yossel had to drag all three of them away from the keys.

The next day was Hyman's Bar Mitzvah. Boris *der Toiber*, Deaf Boris, who helped Papa out on emergencies, came fortified with his hearing aid.

"Don't worry," he yelled. "Between me, the cook, and the dishwasher, the business will be in good hands. *Mazel Tov*. Go and enjoy."

Mama and Papa washed their hands and faces, took off their aprons, and were ready. Hyman, the Bar Mitzvah boy, Bronna, and Rachel went off after them. Uncle Yossel in his *yarmulke* and long, black coat, the only relative representing the family, followed. Then came the customers.

Though it had rained early in the morning, now the sun was shining brightly. The first two lines of the poem Miss Mallory read to the class came to Rachel's mind. She felt like dancing to them.

> April, April, laugh your girlish laughter
> Then the moment after, weep your golden tears.

As they walked quickly along, Rachel took a deep breath of the fresh April breeze. She felt so good. Their little family rarely had a chance to go out together, like other families, especially since Mama and Papa bought the teahouse. How wonderful to be all together like this. How wonderful Uncle Yossel came on this special day. How wonderful of the sun to shine after the early morning rain.

It took no time at all for them to arrive at the Talmud Torah at Third and Catherine Streets, where the Bar Mitzvah was to be observed. She stopped a moment, as always, to look at the tree outside the synagogue. Its branches, heavy with satin-green leaves, stood proudly for her inspection, as if dressed to celebrate this special occasion.

Rachel and her mother and sister went upstairs to the women's section. She searched for Papa, who was downstairs with the men, and quickly sighted him in the first row.

Among the regular congregants, she saw the customers and Hyman's friends filling the seats downstairs. They nodded in greeting to Rachel and her mother and sister.

A handsome, familiar face came into view. It couldn't be. Yes, it was—Benny Kessler! Although he was the same age as her brother, they hadn't been friendly before. Apparently they were now. Hyman never mentioned him. It made the day absolutely complete to see him, to steal as many glimpses of him as she could from her vantage point in the balcony.

A white-faced Hyman in white satin *yarmulke* and prayer shawl stood between the rabbi and cantor at the altar. Because Uncle Yossel was a cantor, the family was honored to have him stand alongside them to chant and pray also. At this long-awaited moment, Rachel trembled for, and with, her brother.

Hyman faltered at first; he could barely be heard. But as the ritual progressed, he became caught up in it, his fears forgotten. Uttering the hallowed words of the *Haftorah*, his voice reached the rafters of the old synagogue. As the service continued, Hyman's voice mingled gloriously with the prayers and singing of the cantors, the rabbi and congregants. Rachel heard him above all the others, even Uncle Yossel.

She saw Papa's face watching Hyman at the *Bimah*. It was aglow. A tender smile danced on his lips, and his eyes shone. Mama tried dutifully to read and keep up with the service, but wept continually, overcome with emotion.

Rachel's heart was full.

Papa was beckoned to the altar. He stood straight and tall, proudly saying the words he had studied for this special moment. As he left, Rachel saw Mama meet his eyes, nodding approvingly.

Soon the ceremony was over. Everyone in the synagogue was invited to the *Kiddush* held in the adjoining room, where Mama and Papa presided over a spread of herring, homemade sponge cake, and wine. Amidst the happy toasts and blessings in his honor, Hyman accepted congratulations on his thirteenth birthday. He had reached the status of a man and was about to assume the duties of manhood.

She saw Ana, looking fresh and lovely in a lavender dress with large scalloped ruffles, and a matching lavender bow in her hair. Ana was talking with, of all people, Benny Kessler. Rachel felt a clamp around her heart. They're only talking, she told herself. It's a free country.

Ana saw her and came right over.

"I didn't know you knew Benny Kessler," said Rachel.

"Oh, I just met him here."

"He's cute, isn't he?"

"If you like that type." Ana's hand stole over to Rachel's. "I'll tell you a secret if you cross your heart to never tell."

"What is it?"

"I think Hyman's much cuter."

Rachel was shocked. Hyman, with his horn-rimmed glasses and big teeth? There was no comparison.

"I've had a crush on him since the day you moved in," Ana said. "He's my secret love. I'm so glad you invited me here."

Rachel was thrilled. She liked Ana better than ever. Perhaps someday she and Ana could walk to Benny Kessler's father's ice cream parlor to see him. She didn't dare look at Benny now. She was too excited. And scared. Then again, maybe she wouldn't seek him out. She'd wait until she became a famous dancer—he would surely love her then.

In the meantime, it was more important to get to dancing school before it was too late. Hyman had just turned thirteen. Before she knew it, she'd be twelve. She had to get those lessons soon.

Rachel heard the rabbi assure Mama and Papa in his deep, resonant voice, "Your son did nicely."

"I could have *plotzed*," said Mama. "He was so perfect."

The customers, sharing in the family pride, gushed, "Hyman was really good. He didn't stumble once."

The cantor said to Uncle Yossel, "Maybe your nephew will become one of us. His voice shows promise. What do you think?"

Everyone waited anxiously for Uncle Yossel's response, especially Mama and Papa, who respected his opinion. They were impressed with the many congregations and choirs he had led as a cantor, as well as his mastery of Hebrew. Since Uncle Yossel was a bachelor and Hyman looked just like him, the boy was obviously his favorite. They did not want Uncle Yossel to be disappointed in Hyman's performance.

Still no answer from Uncle Yossel as everyone awaited his opinion. Then after a long pause, taking a deep breath, his blue eyes afire, in loud, golden tones he announced, "Hyman was superb! He made not one mistake! I never heard better!"

Rachel, her family, the rabbi, cantor, congregants and customers heaved a sigh of relief. Everyone grinned.

It was time to walk back to the teahouse. Uncle Yossel lagged behind everybody, dropping superlatives along the way. "Unbelievable! Wonderful! Tremendous!"

The teahouse had survived the absence of Mama and Papa very nicely, since practically all the customers were at the Bar Mitzvah. After a few minutes discussion of the event, Mama and Papa put on their aprons again, and went back to work.

Uncle Yossel sat outside on the bench mumbling, "Perfect! Splendid! Magnificent!"

Rachel, Hyman, and Bronna raced upstairs. Hyman played the piano rolls, Bronna singing beside him as Rachel danced.

Mama came into the parlor and patted the piano lovingly with her rough, red hands. "Be careful," she said. "Don't scratch the wood."

Uncle Yossel stayed to lead the Passover *seder*. Rachel and her family were looking forward to it, as it had been several years since he had celebrated the holiday with them.

All year round, but especially on the holidays, Rachel envied friends who had cousins by the dozens, watching wistfully as they ran to fat aunts with warm laps or uncles who took them for Sunday car rides. The fact that her uncle, the only relative they had in this country, would be with them at this particular time filled her with great pride. His being a cantor conducting the service would sanctify and make their *seder* more special than anyone else's. As Mama often said, "We may not have quantity, but we have quality."

Getting the teahouse ready for Passover was a gargantuan task. When they lived "private," changing the dishes for the holiday was hard enough. But the undertaking for the store made that effort child's play by comparison.

All the dishes, pots, pans, silverware, and anything that had come in contact with leaven throughout the year had to be removed and put away for after the holiday. Only the special china dishes, pots, and utensils set aside for Passover week were used.

Rachel worked tirelessly with the cook, the dishwasher, and her mother. Even Bronna was called upon to help.

"What a hard job," grunted Bronna.

Rachel wearily agreed.

Mama's face grew grave as she looked up from the array of dishes, pots, and silverware spread out before them to be washed and put away. "Yes, it's lots of work. I remember my mother explaining to me as I helped her why we do this hard job, why we give up bread containing leavening and live on *matzoh*. It's called 'the bread of freedom,' the most important symbol of Passover, made of nothing but flour and water. When our fathers left Egypt so rapidly, they didn't even have time to permit the bread to rise."

The kitchen was very hot. Mama wiped the perspiration on her face with a corner of her apron and continued. "My mother passed the legacy of remembrance to me. I pass it on to you. You, to those who come after you. For one week in springtime we work to remember and recreate Israel's deliverance from slavery over thirty-two hundred years ago."

Mama picked up a pot. "Now, let's get back to work."

In due time, the night of the *seder* arrived. All was ready. After supper business, Papa locked the front door and turned the lights on low. Rachel, in her freshly-washed pink cotton dress, sat down with her family in their table in back of the store for the *seder*. Three other tables had been pulled over to join theirs, because a few special customers had been invited by a last-minute plea from Papa.

"How could we not invite Handfinger? He's our best customer. And Becky, Jake, and Clara—they have nowhere else to go. It's a *mitzvah* to invite them." Before Mama had a

100

chance to answer, he added, "There's Dreyfus, Maxie, Reds, and Dave. We wouldn't be able to buy the teahouse without our extra savings from their card games."

"All right, already, that's eight people. If it was up to you, you'd invite all the customers."

Papa laughed. "That's right, I would." He hesitated. "Also, we have to invite Gedalia, my best friend. You know he just lost his wife and is all alone."

"That's all—nine," Mama declared. "*Oy*, a person could bust from you, Berel."

And so there they were at the long table, clean and sitting at attention with their hands folded. Except there were ten invited besides the family. Papa's friend, Gedalia, the newly bereaved widower, had brought a plump, smiling woman he introduced as his "friend." Mama, her eyes rolling upward in resignation said, "Rachel, please set another place..." She paused, gave one of her deep sighs, and continued, "...for Molly."

There was a soft rap on the door. Mama said, "Berel, don't answer it."

The rap became a loud knocking. Papa went to see who it was. He came back saying, "It's Sam. He looks so forlorn out there. I can't send him away."

"Set another place—that makes eleven," said Mama to Rachel, shrugging her shoulders helplessly. "Seventeen altogether."

Grandmother Rachel's shining candlesticks graced the table covered in white cloths. The symbolic foods of *matzoh*, bitter herbs, roasted egg and bone, *charoseth*, a mixture of chopped nuts, apples, cinnamon, and wine were on the table. Each setting had a wine glass. The *seder*, a combination of banquet and religious service performed at home, was about to begin.

Uncle Yossel in his white satin *yarmulke* and prayer shawl sat at the head of the table. Raising the tray with three *matzohs* on it, showing it to everyone, he recited the opening prayer. "This is the bread of affliction that our fathers ate in the land of Egypt. All who are hungry, let them come and eat—all who are needy, let them come and celebrate Passover with us. Now we are here; next year we may be in Israel. Now we are slaves; in the year ahead we may be free men."

Uncle Yossel raised his wine goblet. "Not only once have they risen to destroy us, but in every generation...But the Holy One, blessed be He, always delivers us from their hands."

Everyone drank of the wine.

As the evening progressed, Rachel noticed how intent everyone was to carefully follow Uncle Yossel's lead. They must be as starved for an authentically Orthodox *seder* as I am, she thought. And who better than Uncle Yossel to lead as he pounded his fists on the table and sang in his golden voice?

She was singularly proud of Bronna. Being the youngest, she had the honor to ask the four questions. As taught in Talmud Torah to say it in Hebrew and then English she asked:

> Why do we eat unleavened bread?
> Why do we use bitter herbs?
> Why do we dip the herbs in salt water?
> Why do we recline at the table?

In reply to the Four Questions, the adults, with Uncle Yossel leading, read from the *Haggadahs*, which explained the symbols as the tale unfolded. "Slaves were we unto Pharaoh in Egypt..." they chanted. The Pharaoh's refusal to let the children of Israel go, the Red Sea parting, Moses receiving the Ten Commandments at Mount Sinai—all the ancient drama of the Exodus was reënacted at the *seder* ceremony.

Rachel loved best the part when, late in the *seder* ritual, a large goblet of wine was poured for the Prophet Elijah, the herald of the Messiah, for his ever hoped-for appearance on earth. "We can't open the front door for him to come in, because we're closed. But we'll open the side door," Mama said. "You never know when he'll come."

During the ceremony, Rachel helped Mama serve the traditional Passover meal courses—a real feast. *Gefilte* fish, chicken liver, chicken soup with matzoh balls, chicken, potato pancakes, and tea to wash it down. There were no leftovers. All the platters were clean.

She was amazed the customers were so well-behaved. Everything went smoothly. At intervals, Clara had to grab Jake's hand when he went for second, third, and fourth helpings. But Papa said, "Let him eat. Let him enjoy." And Rachel couldn't help noticing that when they weren't busy eating, Gedalia and Molly held hands under the table.

At leave-taking, Maxie, Reds, Dreyfus, and Dave, who had been so quiet during the *seder*, were profuse in their gratitude.

Dreyfus, whom Rachel always found so tough, said, "I've never been to a *seder* like this in my whole life. And Yossel's singing was beautiful, even if he didn't sing 'Eli, Eli.' Such a golden voice!"

Though he turned his head, she actually saw him wipe a tear away from his eye.

"I loved it," said Reds. "It took me back to my child-hood."

"Me, too," said Maxie. "A privilege. A night to remember."

Rachel realized as she looked at Maxie, who was very short, that as they grew taller, he seemed to get shorter.

"Thanks for inviting us," Dave said, kissing Mama's hand. Carried away with this bit of gallantry, he lifted her for a kiss on the cheek. The Adam's apple in his throat wobbled more furiously than ever. Rachel hoped this strenuous exertion wouldn't prove too much for him. Mama weighed about a hundred and sixty pounds. Dave looked no more than a hundred pounds.

Handfinger lingered at the door silently, then blurted, "It was wonderful. Do me something, I feel like you're the family I never had."

Sam, the last to leave, wheezed, "You are blessed with a good woman, Berel. If I had one like her, I'd never have gotten sick and sold the teahouse."

To Rachel's surprise, he continued with Solomon's Proverb that Mama had taught her. "'A woman of worth—who can find her? For her price is above rubies. The heart of her husband trusteth in her.'" He patted Papa on the shoulder. "That's the kind of woman you have, Berel."

Rachel thought someday she'd have a family and a *seder* like Mama's, and be a woman of worth, also. Plus a dancer, of course!

CHAPTER THIRTEEN

The long-awaited Friday of the tryout finally arrived.

At breakfast, which Rachel hardly touched, Bronna, Hyman, Papa, and all the customers wished her luck. Mama beckoned for her to come into the kitchen.

"Rachel," she said, "I want you to know why I've been stern about you and your dancing."

"Please, Mama, not today—not now," Rachel protested, attempting to leave.

Her mother took her hand. "I did all I could to stop you."

"But why, Mama? Why?"

"I didn't want you to get hurt. I know the pain."

"How could you?"

"When I was young like you, I, too, wanted to be a dancer."

Rachel stared at Mama in shocked disbelief. In all her stories about her youth, she had never mentioned it. Mama in her shapeless dresses and oversized aprons. Where was the grace, the movement?

"I never had a chance. I know what it is to give up a dream. I wanted to spare you—yet wanted you to have what I couldn't." A tear shone in Mama's eye as she continued, "These are different times—a woman has more choices. She can have a husband, a family, and a career."

Her mother took her in her arms. "I was wrong. Misguided. You must have a chance at your dream. I give you my blessing."

Rachel saw Papa glance her way. He smiled and nodded approvingly to Mama, apparently aware of their conversation. She left for school, her heart lighter now that she understood Mama's mixed feelings about her dancing.

Nevertheless, she was anxious and jittery in class. When the dismissal bell rang, she jumped out of her seat. The other students laughed.

As she filed out with the rest of the class, Miss Mallory's eyes caught hers. Her lips mouthed the words, "Good luck."

Ana was waiting in the corridor. "I'll walk with you to the Center," she said.

"It's all right—you don't have to."

"I can help carry some of your books and dancing stuff."

"Thanks anyway. I'd rather go by myself," said Rachel. She clutched her bag containing a blouse, a pair of shorts, and her ballet slippers.

Ana seemed reluctant to leave. Was there hurt in her eyes?

Rachel felt a twinge of guilt as she left her friend standing alone. She remembered how patiently Ana had listened to her while she talked of nothing else but the upcoming tryout, and how grateful she'd been when Ana helped her with fractions, making them seem easier. She was also pleased because Ana had confided her crush on Hyman to her, of all people. But now that the crucial time for the audition was here, she wanted to speed away by herself. She hoped Ana would understand.

She'd gone but a few steps when there was a tap on her shoulder. It was Ana. Rachel looked at her.

"I wanted to wish you good luck," Ana whispered. "I envy you being able to dance. I can't. I've always been such a *klutz*." She gave Rachel a quick kiss on the cheek and darted away.

Rachel watched Ana's retreating form in utter amazement. Ana envied her? Ana, of the beautiful dresses, each one with a sash tied in a beautiful bow in back, and a matching hair ribbon. Ana, who had answers to the questions in class. Whose parents' fancy restaurant—with the white tablecloths—made Mama and Papa's teahouse seem poor. Ana envied her?

Imagine! Ana longed for things Rachel took for granted. Ana, an only child, wished she had a brother and sister. Perhaps that was why her secret love was Hyman, Rachel's brother.

But Ana couldn't dance. Rachel couldn't imagine anyone not being able to dance. Even a little. Dance lent itself to her every movement; it was as natural to her as breathing. Her world of silver and gold.

You never know when you look at a person on the outside, what they're really like on the inside. Why, she was rich compared to Ana. She would try to teach Ana to dance. Maybe she'd even tell her that Benny Kessler was *her* secret love.

With no thought of anything but the audition, Rachel practically ran the five blocks to the Arts Center. When she arrived, the woman at the desk referred her to Room 213. She entered a large room with a long barre on one side and full length mirrors covering the other wall directly opposite.

The only furniture was a small piano in a corner of the room, and a table where a woman sat, dressed in black. Rachel was surprised there was no one else. She heard the woman call to her. "Do you want the dance class?"

"Yes," said Rachel, hearing the echo of her voice bounce back. She had a strange feeling that this moment she so longed for was not real. Just another of her impossible dreams.

The woman rose and came toward her, each step dispelling the illusion of fantasy. Rachel heard her voice clear as crystal, "I'm Miss Baker, the dance teacher. Come in."

Rachel couldn't help staring. Miss Baker was the tiniest woman she'd ever seen. She walked with floating grace. Her shiny white face contrasted sharply with the black hair, black leotard, black tights, and pink ballet slippers.

"What is your name?" the bell-like voice asked.

"I'm Rachel Sussman. I'm here to apply for a dance scholarship." She produced the card signed by her father.

Miss Baker's black eyes scanned the card, then Rachel. "It's good you got here early. The beginner's class is from four to five, and the advanced from five to six. Have you ever had dance lessons?"

"No."

"You'll take the beginner's class and try out for the scholarship."

Rachel listened attentively, her eyes devouring Miss Baker. Her silky black hair was parted in the middle, pulled down in a straight sweep over her ears, then securely tied in a bun at the nape of her neck. She looked exactly as Rachel always imagined a ballerina should.

"You can use the dressing room to change, and then come back," said Miss Baker, pointing to an adjoining room.

Rachel walked into the room and saw several girls seated on wooden benches, undressing. They glanced up at her for a moment, then continued. She was pushed farther into the room by two girls coming in closely behind her, and she sat down with a thump on the nearest bench.

The clock on the wall read ten minutes to four. She realized she should hurry, but there was so much to see. More girls entered the crowded room. Some her age, some younger, and some older.

"Hi, Mary, Hi, Sally," they greeted each other, amidst kissing, hugging and giggling. She watched avidly, listening to the combined voices and breathing in the mingled aroma of bodies. She held tight to the moment, as if in an embrace.

The girl next to her on the bench asked, "This is your first time here, isn't it?"

Rachel managed a startled, "Uh-huh," surprised she noticed.

"I didn't think I saw you here before. And I can tell the way you're looking around, you're new. You better hurry. Miss Baker starts her class promptly at four; she doesn't like anyone to be late."

"Thanks." In Rachel's dazed state she could only speak one word at a time.

"Just put your things together on the bench, that's where everyone leaves them," said the girl as she rose, adding, "Bye."

Rachel noticed the girls undressed in front of each other unashamedly. Although she was embarrassed to see the girls' budding breasts, she couldn't help staring. She examined her breasts every night in the mirror to see if they were growing, but they still looked like two pink pimples. Slipping out of her dress, she held it up in front of her, as a shield, while putting on her shorts and blouse. She tied the blouse together in a bow at her waist, as she saw the other girls do, and put on her ballet slippers.

Several girls were lined up, vying to get in front of the small mirror on the wall to fix their hair. They all had long hair which they pulled straight over their ears and rolled into a bun at the neck, just like Miss Baker's. Her hand automatically went up to give her straight, short hair a pat. She resolved immediately to let it grow, so she could wear it that way also.

She was now ready and flew off to the dancing class. Miss Baker was talking to two women, one standing next to her and one seated at the piano. Rachel walked towards them. Undecided whether to interrupt the conversation, she stopped and stood a short distance away.

The room, which had seemed so large when it was empty, now appeared smaller with all the girls in it. Some were exercising at the barre, others talking in groups of twos and threes. The rest watched themselves in the mirror as they practiced. She quickly counted sixteen girls. With the few still in the dressing room, they totaled about twenty-two.

Miss Baker signaled to Rachel with her index finger to come forward. "Mrs. Jones is our accompanist, and Miss Daisy, my assistant on the floor." Miss Baker stopped as Rachel returned their smiles of acknowledgment. "The class is going to start now. I want you up front."

The pianist struck a few loud chords for attention. Miss Baker announced, "Class will begin."

Rachel noticed although Miss Baker spoke to the entire class, she looked directly at her. "Every girl dreams of becoming a ballerina. The grace, the beauty, it is a romantic, lovely world that appeals to a young heart. You are here to learn. In ballet dancing there is a certain order. Just as a baby must stand before it learns to walk, and walk before it can run, the serious student of dancing has to learn the foundations of ballet before going on to the more dramatic and complicated steps."

Rachel's eyes never left Miss Baker's. Her heart rejoiced as the words filled the air. They were words she had hungered to hear, words she had seen printed on the pages of the dance books she'd read. Now, leaping out like music from Miss Baker's lips, they welcomed her to this world she loved.

"With the help of this class you can learn the first exercises in ballet dancing. They are the basics. The most famous ballerinas limber up every day with these exact routines. The important thing is to master your technique, and practice, practice, every day."

Rachel was inspired. If she could only win the scholarship, remain in class. She would work harder than ever, practice more than ever, dedicate herself to learn, to finally attain her dream.

"And now, class—to the barre." Miss Baker finished her speech.

The girls scrambled to their places, Rachel remembering to take hers in front of Miss Baker, as instructed. The pianist started to play a lovely Viennese waltz and Miss Daisy stood to the side, smiling at them. At last, I begin, thought Rachel.

"Remember," Miss Baker said, "a dancer always carries her body as if she is dancing, even when she is walking down the street or sleeping in bed. She *is* dance. And that is why she is so beautiful." She stopped to point to a girl. "Alice, you are slouching." Then to another girl, "Irene, keep your stomach in. This is what I'm talking about. Posture is all-important."

Rachel immediately straightened her back and pulled in her stomach, feeling the same imperceptible movement made by the other girls down the line.

Miss Baker was saying, "All that we do today we do over and over again at each class, to perfect our technique. Dancing is not just legs and feet. It uses the whole body, especially the arms which must move smoothly, gracefully, and expressively. First I will demonstrate the position and then the class will follow.

"Place your left hand on the barre," Miss Baker said, her left hand slowly and delicately touching the barre. "Now raise your right arm to the side." Rachel marveled at the soft curve of Miss Baker's arm.

"Turn your toes outward as far as you comfortably can, your heels touching. Try to turn your leg out all the way from your hip, instead of just pointing the toe forward. This is known as the 'turn-out' and the better a dancer's turn-out, the better she will dance."

Rachel was entranced as she studied the bird-like grace of Miss Baker's every movement, hung on her every word.

"Now, class—first position," Miss Baker ordered. Along with the rest of the class, Rachel got into the position she had practiced at home so many times. Heels together and both feet completely turned out to form a single straight line, she stood poised, her head erect. Miss Baker picked out certain students and shouted to them, "Keep your shoulders down. Keep your back straight."

Rachel heard Miss Baker call her name. "Rachel, turn your leg out from the hip."

Miss Daisy came to Rachel and straightened out her leg.

"That's better," said Miss Baker.

"Next is second position," said Miss Baker, demonstrating by holding both feet in the same line as for the first position, but adding a space between them.

Rachel watched, taking in every detail, remembering to keep her weight evenly on both feet and in a straight line under her body. Miss Baker's eyes rested on her for a moment, but she did not say a word, encouraging or otherwise, although she continued to call out suggestions and corrections to the other girls, directing Miss Daisy to help them.

Rachel felt her tension and fear melt away. She came to try for the scholarship and would do her very best. Most of all, she was dancing in a class, at last, and loving every moment of it.

They went through all the five positions, which Rachel knew by heart, first with the right leg, then with the left, and the mirror told her she was doing them correctly.

Next followed a series of exercises: *pliés, battement tendus*, ending with the stretching. All the terms were familiar to Rachel from the illustrations in books and her self-imposed practice.

They spread out in the center of the classroom and began to practice the barre exercises without the barre. Rachel knew that these movements, *port de bras, pirouettes*, and *adagio*, helped improve balance and strength.

Occasionally, Miss Daisy approached her to straighten a leg or smooth her arm, smiling approvingly.

But Miss Baker said nothing more to Rachel.

Rachel's senses were tingling, thrilled by the reality of hearing Miss Baker pronounce the French terms, and watching her perform. Following the movements with the rest of the class was like being awake in a dream. For the last and most exhilarating part of class they moved across the floor in pairs. As Rachel executed the jumping and leaping combinations, she felt as if she could dance on and on and on. Oh, how she wished the class would never end.

But it finally did. The class bowed in acknowledgment to the teachers and were dismissed. The girls hurriedly left for the dressing room in a clamor of buzzing voices and laughter. Rachel stood stock-still in her last position, savoring the last note on the piano, the last moment in class.

Miss Daisy and Miss Baker came toward her. Miss Daisy, of average height, looked like a tall, thin scarecrow next to Miss Baker, flitting about like a tiny blackbird beside her.

Miss Daisy gently lifted Rachel up from her curtsy. Patting her on the shoulder, she said with a big smile, "You did very well for the first time. I like your turn-outs."

Up close, Rachel saw a spattering of brown freckles on the bridge of Miss Daisy's nose. Her yellow hair framed her face and friendly brown eyes, the same colors as in a daisy, making her name perfectly suitable. There was even a scent of fresh flowers about her. Rachel actually began to see a daisy.

It was nice that Miss Daisy was so encouraging. But, Rachel reminded herself, she was merely an assistant. Miss Baker decided who got the scholarship.

Miss Baker cleared her throat. Lips pursed, black eyes narrowed, she looked Rachel up and down. Rachel suddenly realized she had not seen Miss Baker smile, not even once, at her. Perhaps her teacher didn't like her. Rachel's heart began to beat louder and louder. Panicky, she thought—what if she didn't get the scholarship?

Rachel took a deep breath to calm herself. A vision of Mama lighting the Sabbath candles in her grandmother's silver candlesticks came to her. She saw the flame leaping higher and higher, as though keeping pace with her quickened heartbeats. And she heard a voice from deep within, perhaps the part of her that was Bubbe Rachel herself saying, "Have courage. Don't be afraid. If you don't get this scholarship, something else will turn up. Hold your head high and have faith in yourself."

The flame from the candles danced even higher as Papa's words strengthened her. "With God's help, if you want something bad enough, hard enough, you will find a way to make your dream come true."

And she envisioned Mama shrugging her shoulders, saying, "Rachel, grow up. How you make your bed, that's how you'll lie in it."

For the first time, she understood it was up to her to make things come to pass, just as she had made this moment happen. Wishing alone wouldn't do it. And no matter what today's outcome, she would not give up or be afraid to try again. It would never be too late for her. Her dream would burn steadfastly, as the golden fire in the candle, until she could find a way to make it come true.

Rachel's nervousness subsided. She felt strangely calm as she looked into Miss Baker's unsmiling eyes and finally heard her speak.

"Did you say you never took dance lessons, Rachel?"

"Yes."

"How do you know all the movements?"

"From movies and pictures in library books. I practice at home by myself."

Miss Baker's brows knit. She exchanged looks with Miss Daisy.

"Well, keep practicing," said Miss Baker. She spoke slowly, looking very serious. Not a hint of a smile.

Rachel's heart sank. But she kept her head high, remembering, come what may, that she would not give up. This would not break her.

Miss Baker continued. "You have talent. You couldn't do what you do, if you didn't. But talent alone is not enough. There's lots of study and hard work to being a ballerina. Dedication."

Miss Baker paused. The silence hung heavy in the large, empty room.

"And, yes," she heard Miss Baker say. "You can come back next Friday."

Rachel's heart raced. Incredulous, she looked at Miss Baker.

She saw the light of the moon, the stars, the sky lit up in Miss Baker's black eyes. Her lips, parting in a smile as dazzlingly bright as the sun, delivered the words, "You have the scholarship."

Rachel felt sparks of joy burst into a million fragments inside of her. So this is what it feels like when a dream comes true?

She wanted to shout and clap her hands and jump up and down. Instead, she bowed before the teacher and felt as though she were accepting the applause of thousands.

Rachel remembered that spellbound evening with Papa at the ballet. The beauty—the magic. How she'd vowed somehow, some way she would be part of that world.

She looked into Miss Baker's eyes and quietly said, "Thank you."

She was on her way.

Thank you dear God, thank you for answering my prayers, Rachel chanted as she danced all the way home, eager to tell her family the news: Mama and Papa, Bronna, Hyman, and yes, the customers—they were family, too. She couldn't wait to tell Ana and Miss Mallory. Shout it out to the world.

Bubbe Rachel danced beside her.

And Mama did, too.

.

Made in the USA
Middletown, DE
13 December 2022

18497501R00070